BOOK gIRL

and the Suicidal Mime

Mizuki Nomura

KONOHA INOUE

Nothing happening.
Not having a crush on anybody.
I could live in peace, without pain, or sadness, or disappointment.

I prayed that every day would be that way, for the rest of my life.

TOHKO AMANO

This is why you have to watch your back around book girls.
Their minds are full of literature without any concept of
reality, so if you take your eyes off them, there's no telling
what mischief they'll get into. They'll drag other people into
their schemes without even a twinge of regret

BOOK GIRL AND THE SUICIDAL MIME

002

Konoha Inoue

Today's Snack, by Inoue Konoha

Tohko Amano

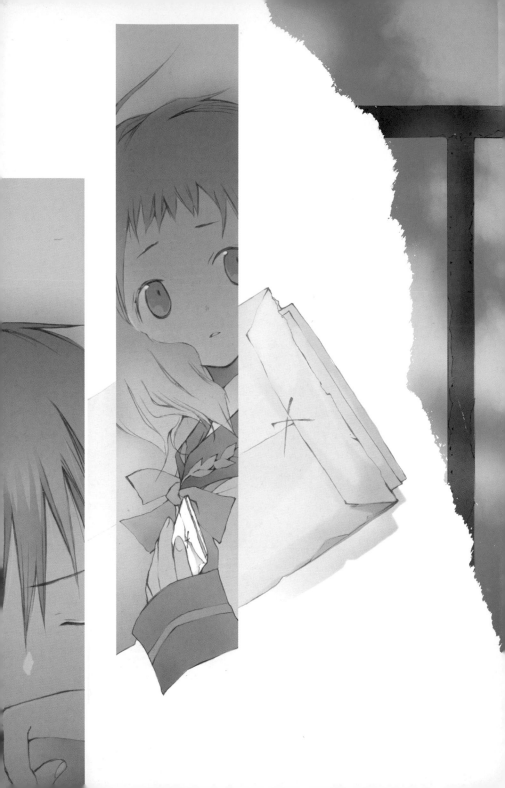

Mine has been a life of shame.
I'm ashamed.

Ashamed to be alive.

That day, I had killed a person.
I doubt that God will ever forgive me.

Contents

BOOK giRL

and the Suicidal Mime

Volume 1

Mizuki Nomura

Yen Press

NEW YORK

BOOK GIRL AND THE SUICIDAL MIME
MIZUKI NOMURA

Translation by Karen McGillicuddy

Bungakushoujo to shinitagari no pierrot ©2006 Mizuki
Nomura. All rights reserved. First published in Japan in
2006 by ENTERBRAIN, INC., Tokyo. English translation
rights arranged with ENTERBRAIN, INC. through Tuttle-
Mori Agency, Inc., Tokyo.

English translation © 2010 by Hachette Book Group, Inc.

Yen Press
Hachette Book Group
237 Park Avenue, New York, NY 10017

Visit our websites at www.HachetteBookGroup.com and
www.YenPress.com.

Yen Press is an imprint of Hachette Book Group, Inc. The
Yen Press name and logo are trademarks of Hachette Book
Group, Inc.

First Yen Press Edition: July 2010

Library of Congress Cataloging-in-Publication Data

Nomura, Mizuki.
    [Bungakushoujo to shinitagari no pierrot. English]
    Book girl and the suicidal mime / Mizuki Nomura ;
Illustrations by Miho Takeoka. — 1st Yen Press ed.
      p. cm.
    Summary: While attending their book club meetings,
Japanese high school students, Konoha and Tohko, who
is actually a literature-eating goblin in disguise, uncover a
mystery surrounding the death of a former student.
    ISBN 978-0-316-07690-6
    [1. Mystery and detective stories.   2. Books and
reading—Fiction.   3. Goblins—Fiction.   4. Japan—
Fiction.]   I. Takeoka, Miho, ill.   II. Title.
    PZ7.N728Bo 2010
    [Fic]—dc22

                                              2009054209

ISBN: 978-0-316-07690-6

10 9 8 7 6 5 4 3 2 1

RRD-C

Printed in the United States of America

Mizuki Nomura

Mine has been a life of shame.

I'm like the one black sheep born into a pure white flock.
Unable to enjoy the things my peers enjoyed, unable to
grieve the things they grieved, unable to eat the things they
ate—being born an ignoble black sheep, I didn't understand
the things my friends found pleasant, such as love, kindness,
and sympathy. I simply dusted my dark wool in white powder
and pretended I was a white sheep, too.

I'm still wearing my mask, still acting in this farce.

Prologue – Memories for an Introduction—Volume 1: The Author, Girl Prodigy

Mine has been a life of shame.

Hold on—who's that talking? An actor? An athlete? A politician who was arrested for corruption?

Well, whatever.

Maybe it's a little overblown to talk about my life so dramatically since I only just started my second year of high school. But the things I experienced at fourteen turned my world upside down. Trial followed on tribulation, which was followed by bursts of outright craziness, and in one short year, I felt as if my life had come to an end.

Why? Because during that year, the eyes of all Japan were on me: a brilliant, mysterious author who happened to be a lovely young girl.

It all started in the spring of my last year of middle school.

I was fourteen-soon-to-be-fifteen, living the life of a perfectly ordinary middle school boy. I had friends, had a girl that I liked, and the kind of fun you'd expect someone with those things to have. An impulse made me submit the first novel I'd ever written to a literary magazine for a new author competition. I won the grand prize and was the youngest winner ever, to boot.

My narrator was a young girl, and my pen name was Miu Inoue—a girl's name—so I got a ton of publicity with headlines such as "Youngest Winner Ever! 14-Year-Old Girl Takes the Prize!" or "In a Unanimous Decision, Realistic Style and Refreshing Sensitivity!"

God, I'm so embarrassed.

My publisher ran with it. "People are more receptive to girls, so let's go ahead with the mysterious young girl as a masked author to sell it."

I didn't quite get how people would know the author was a cute little girl if she was wearing a mask, but they published the award-winning story, which quickly became a best seller. The book was flying out of stores, and it soon shattered the one-million-copies-sold mark. It was adapted into a movie and a TV miniseries, and there was also a comic book adaptation. It became a phenomenon.

I was astounded.

My family didn't know what to think.

"My son? Well…he used to be such a nice, ordinary boy. What can we do? The royalties are a billion yen! I mean, that's twenty times his father's salary!"

They were in shock.

Whenever I got on the train, the ads for my book were staring me in the face, the title printed in gigantic letters. And if I so much as set foot in a bookstore, I saw my book stacked up on the checkout counters like stalwart fortresses with big-name reviews on the covers.

"Little Miu is still in middle school, right? I wonder what she's like. I bet she's cute."

"I heard she's a rich kid from an old, aristocratic family. That's why they can't say who she really is."

"She must have been raised by nannies since she was a baby. She's probably never had to lift anything heavier than a pen."

"Oh, definitely. She just screams 'book girl.' You just know she's a delicate, innocent young lady. God, Miu, I want you so bad! Marry me!"

Whenever I heard people saying these things, I got so embarrassed it felt like I was suffocating. I only cared about getting away.

I'm *so* sorry, please don't get mad at me, it was just a whim, my story's not some great work of literature. They were just scribbles in my notes for class that somehow won an award. I'm really sorry. I could never hope to have "refreshing sensitivity." It's just the ramblings of a boring, wimpy little kid. The illustrious members of the judging panel were only trying to make a joke. They were just thinking, *Hey, wouldn't it be funny if a fourteen-year-old girl won the prize? Wouldn't that be incredible PR material? And it would give the industry a real shot in the arm, too. I bet it would sell like crazy. That would make the publishers happy.* They gave in to temptation. I have no talent whatsoever. Please, please forgive me, I'm so sorry.

I yearned to go to every last corner of Japan and throw myself at people's feet to apologize, until finally *it* happened—the stress made me hyperventilate, and I passed out at school and got taken to the hospital. I was sobbing pathetically about how I couldn't write novels anymore, and I even refused to go to school. I put my parents and my little sister through a lot.

Have I mentioned how embarrassing that year was?

That was how the mysterious genius, the masked young author, Miu Inoue, burned out after producing only one novel. I took my exams, passed them, and started high school, which is where I met a real "book girl"—an older girl named Tohko Amano.

Why did I start writing again?

Because I met Tohko under the brilliant white magnolia trees that day.

Chapter 1 – Tohko Has Refined Tastes

"Gallico's story feels like winter to me. It's like the purity of falling snow melting on your tongue—the serenity you get from that coolness and ephemerality. It has that same beauty and desolation to it." Tohko sighed with pleasure as she flipped through a collection of Paul Gallico's stories.

We belonged to the Seijoh Academy book club, which met in the western corner of the school's third floor.

As the day ended, the sun lit the room with a beguiling golden light the color of honey.

An old oak table stood in the middle of the tiny room, which was mainly used for storage and smelled of old paper and dust. Cardboard boxes were stacked to dizzying heights along the walls. There were also two steel bookshelves and a locker. That filled the room to bursting, so we stacked old books we had no space for on every available surface. If there was ever an earthquake, the towers of books would probably topple over and bury us alive.

Tohko was perched on a metal folding chair, her knees pulled up to her chest. It wasn't a very modest way for her to sit. Her pleated skirt was *almost* wide open—but not quite. If she moved her legs even slightly she would be flashing me.

She rested a pale cheek on her bare knees and wound one arm around her legs so she could turn lovingly through the book with her slender fingers.

Her dark bangs fell across the white skin of her forehead and trailing braids fell over her shoulder to her hips. The whiteness of her skin made the black of her hair, her eyebrows, and her eyes stand out.

When she was quiet, Tohko seemed incredibly refined. Like a living doll.

But then... she slowly tore a page out of the book, *stuffed it into her mouth*, and started chewing it like a goat.

God, she's eating it... That never gets any less surreal.

R-r-rip, crinkle, flupp.

Nom-nom-nom—gulp.

Her slender throat made an adorable sound as she swallowed the page. She ripped out and ate another page, her placid expression transforming as her eyes closed with joy. She beamed.

"Gallico really is de-*lic*ious. Did you know he was born in New York? Everybody knows him for the movie *The Poseidon Adventure* and the *Mrs. Harris* series of children's books, but if you ask me, his best story has to be *The Snow Goose*. It's all about the poignant connection between two quiet souls, a lonely painter named Rhayader who lives in a lighthouse next to a marsh, and a girl named Fritha who appears one day carrying an injured white goose. Words are powerless to describe the deep affection they have for each other. Ah—their love is so pure!

"Got that, Konoha? You shouldn't just ramble on and on. You have to carry the truly important emotions with you to the grave. It's the struggle to not speak of things that gives them poignancy and beauty. The last scene makes me cry every time I read it. Gallico's stories are like an exquisite sorbet, soothing your burning passion. It feels amazing, sliding sweetly down my throat! You've

got to read *Jennie* and *Snowflake*, too. And if it's not Sumiko Yagawa's translation, don't bother."

I was at the lopsided table writing an improv story in a notebook with a mechanical pencil.

Words were spilling onto the page, so I kept my eyes down and coolly interjected, "It tastes like sorbet? Tohko, you're a goblin. Writing is the only thing you can taste. How can you compare it to anything?"

Tohko pouted at me for that.

"Why not? I can imagine it just fine! I can say, 'Oh, sorbet must taste like *this!*' Besides, 'goblin' is a slur. I'm just a book girl: a pretty high school student like any other, who loves all the stories and literature of the world so intensely that she devours them."

"I don't think most high school girls rip pages out to nibble on, though. Or at least, you're the only weirdo like that I ever heard of in the sixteen years I've been around."

Tohko puffed her cheeks out even more. "You're awful! How can you call a girl a weirdo to her face? That hurts. You look so nice on the surface, like you would keep roses at home and name them things like Nancy and Betty and take really good care of them, but I think you're lacking a little in delicacy toward your elders."

"Wait, *you* think *I* lack delicacy?"

"What's that supposed to mean?" Tohko grumbled. But her mood recovered almost immediately. She hopped out of her chair and leaned forward with a coy look in her eyes. "Well, never mind. My compassion is as vast as the Andromeda Galaxy, so I'll overlook one or two rude comments from an upstart kid. More important, is my treat ready yet?" she asked excitedly.

She was such an uncomplicated person. If she were a cat, she would have been purring.

One year my senior, Tohko Amano is the president of the book club—and also a goblin who eats stories.

9

Instead of eating bread and drinking water, she gobbles up pages from books and any paper with writing on it.

One year ago, I don't know how, this book girl with the long braids dragged me into the book club, and ever since then as soon as classes were over, she would pester me. "I'm hunnngryyy," she says. "C'mon, write something. Pleeease?" And I slap together a poem or an essay for her.

Even now that it's May and I've moved up to the second year, Tohko and I are still the only two people in the book club. Just the other day, Tohko was upset about the fact that not a single first-year student showed up.

"Take these, Konoha. This is a direct order from your president!"

And, lagging behind the times a little, she shoved some recruitment flyers into my hands. I passed them out, my face burning the whole time I stood outside the school gates, but it didn't look like any new members were going to come.

I wonder if I can stay with this club if it's just me and this freakish president.

Why am I in the book club anyway, of all things, after I swore I would never write another novel? I was supposed to be through with writing of any kind.

And now writing little snack stories for my weird goblin president isn't even strange anymore. It's become totally normal.

Tohko took a silver stopwatch from her pocket and showed it to me.

"Look, you only have five minutes left. Write an absolutely delicious snack for your beloved president. Gallico had a restrained, refreshing sweetness, so now I want something *dripping* with sugar. A poignant story would be great, too, but love stories should have happy endings, after all. Don't do anything where the love interest dies from leukemia or a weak heart or in a plane

crash or from choking on a strawberry mochi or anything like that."

Got it.

Plot twist—I'd make him run into the first girl he ever loved on the steps of the Diet Building and then have a box of strawberry mochi fall out of the sky and kill her.

Tohko leaned on the table, chin in her hand, grinning.

At first glance, she seemed like a low-key beauty, but when she was waiting for food, she became a full-blown pig and acted like a total brat. Her black eyes flashed with expectation.

"Mmm, I just *love* handwritten stories. Ōgai and Soseki have a finely crafted flavor when you read them in books, but amateurs have their own charming naiveté. Especially when it's hand-written. I feel as if I'm dipping my hands into a gurgling stream to take a drink. It's like biting into a freshly picked tomato or cucumber or something! Even the little tastes of grit just *blow* my *mind!*"

So I write like tomatoes and cucumbers...

I wondered what she would do if I told her that two years ago I was that mysterious girl who won a prize for new authors and became a best seller.

But of course nothing would *actually* make me say that.

"Only two minutes left! One last push! You can do it!"

Tohko cheered me on. She angled her slender neck to peer up at me eagerly.

I got you now, Tohko. Things aren't gonna go as smoothly as you think.

Just then we heard a voice.

"Hellooo, is anybody in? Ack!"

The moment the door opened, we heard a thud and someone fell into the room.

A girl was splayed out on the floor, her skirt flipped up in her fall, exposing her bear-print underwear for all to see. It occurred to me that my little sister had the exact same pair of underwear, but she was only just starting elementary school.

The girl picked herself up, groaning noisily. But as she reached out a hand, she brushed against one of the towers of books, which immediately collapsed on top of her, and she dove to the ground again.

"Waugh!"

Bang!

"Muh...mah nothe (my nose)...mah nothe (my nose)..."

The girl was twitching slightly, her hands pressed to her nose. Tohko rushed over to her.

"Don't look, Konoha!"

She quickly fixed the girl's skirt to hide her underwear, but I'd already seen it. Besides, I wasn't such a perv that I would get aroused by bear-print underwear.

"Are you all right?"

Tohko put an arm around the girl and helped her up. As soon as she was on her feet, the girl crumpled back down into a little ball and turned a bright, undignified red.

"Y-yeth, thankth. I fall down a lot. I'm really good at falling down in empty rooms. Don't worry, I'm used to it."

I wouldn't call that being "good" at something.

"Um, my name is Chia Takeda. I'm a first-year student in the second class. I came to see the book club for a *super* important request."

She was a small, chubby girl with a cloud of hair that fell to the tops of her shoulders. She was sort of reminiscent of a miniature dachshund or a toy poodle. Something like that.

Could she be a prospective new member? Had the leaflets Tohko

13

made me hand out actually paid off? If so, that was great. If we got a junior member, I could foist Tohko's snack duty off on her.

As soon as I had latched on to this faint hope, Takeda clasped her hands together and beseeched us in a voice packed with resolve, "Please grant me my love!"

My mouth fell open.

"Uh, you know we're the book club, right?"

Takeda turned to me and nodded firmly. "I do! I saw your mailbox!"

"Our mailbox...?" I had no clue what she was talking about.

"There's a mailbox tucked under a tree in a back corner of the schoolyard. It looks like it's hiding! A sign on it says 'We will grant you your love. Interested parties, please send us a letter. By, the Book Club' and it was definitely like a *thud!* or a *zzzap!* or anyway, like a sign from heaven. I figured I didn't have time to write a letter, so I ran straight here."

Despite my astonishment, I suddenly understood what had happened. "Tohko!"

No one but her would do something so outrageous.

Tohko laid a hand on Takeda's shoulder and smiled at her. "It's a good thing you came. I'm the club president, Tohko Amano. You just leave everything to us."

I stood up behind her and shouted, "Hold on! Are you including me in that 'us'?"

"Yes, I am. The *entire book club* is going to do everything they can to support little Chia in her romance."

"Gosh, I really appreciate it!"

"Are you kidding me? Urgggh."

"In exchange, we have one condition," Tohko informed her gently, clamping a hand over my mouth. "Once your love has been achieved, we want you to turn in a full love report, thoroughly detailing how it all happened."

"Oh no, really? A report? I'm pretty awful at writing."

"That's fine. All you have to do is write down the things that happened and how you felt, exactly the way you experienced it. As long as you try your very best, the honest words of someone who doesn't usually write can inspire the heart and the appetite so much more than works that rely on technical mastery. Write down your every thought proudly and give us a delectable story—I mean, report. Oh, and you can't use a computer! You have to write it *by hand* on clean paper. Promise?"

Tohko linked her slender finger with Takeda's, sealing an exuberant pinky-promise.

So that was her goal all along.

Unsatisfied with having only the snacks that I wrote for her, Tohko was so food-obsessed that she had masterminded the idea to set up a relationship advice box and extort steamy reports from the people who came for help.

If all she had done was think it up, that would have been fine. But putting it so brazenly into practice required a particularly Tohko-esque reason.

This is why you have to watch your back around book girls.

Their minds are full of literature without any concept of reality, so if you take your eyes off them, there's no telling what mischief they'll get into. They'll drag other people into their schemes without even a twinge of regret.

"Okay! I'll try real hard and write lots of reports!"

I just couldn't believe how submissive Takeda's personality was (though if it weren't, she never would have come to this questionable club after seeing that shady mailbox). Her eyes sparkled as she gazed up at Tohko. I could just imagine her thinking, *She's so amazing and trustworthy!*

Puffing up her flat-as-a-table A-cup (give or take) chest importantly, Tohko said, "Heh-heh. You just put your mind at ease.

We've studied romance novels old and new, the world over. We're love experts, but also masters of the written word. We'll write the best love letter the world has ever seen for you, Chia. Konoha here can handle it."

"What?!"

Fed up with Tohko's unflagging hunger for fine dining, I had been playing dumb this whole time, but that got me.

"I'll have Konoha think up something good. He's our *top* guy; one of his letters will shoot an arrow straight through the heart of your beloved, Chia."

"I didn't agree to this, Tohko! I've never written a love letter."

Tohko covered my mouth for this last part, so I'm sure all Takeda heard were muffled cries.

"Konoha is our love letter specialist. He's written hundreds of them, and he thinks you'll be impressed. Konoha is a champ. He made it to the final round of the Adatara Literature of Love competition."

What kind of no-name competition is that? It sounds like something even locals wouldn't have heard of.

"Oh wow, that's amazing! It's so exciting that such a great writer is going to write my letters for me!"

Hey, I'm *not* a writer!

Well, I mean, I guess I *was* a writer...and I *was* a best seller... But still! Now I'm just an ordinary high school student, just Tohko's snack-maker, and there's no way I could write love letters for someone else.

While I was lost in thought, the conversation wrapped up without me.

"Thank you, Konoha!"

"Sure thing. It'll be a cinch, right, Konoha?"

And so I pretended to be a girl—again—and wrote the love letters.

Addendum

After Takeda left, Tohko let out a little sob as she ate the improv story I had written for her.

"Oh, grooooss! A box of strawberry mochi fell on his first love and killed her! Blech, blech! This tastes weird! It's like miso soup with jelly beans in it! Blech! Ppth! Soooo gross!"

Chapter 2 – The Most Delicious Story in the World

My grandmother's death was the first incident that showed me I was out of step with the rest of the world.

She'd been very fond of me. Even after an illness in her chest meant that she did little other than sleep, she wanted me by her side. She stroked my hair and called me "such a good boy, such a kind boy," her eyes crinkling with happiness.

But I wasn't the simple child my grandmother wished me to be. Her emaciated hands, her face guttered by wrinkles, her white, whispering husks of hair, her breath that reeked of medicine—all of it repelled and frightened me.

"You're a good boy, a kind boy."

Each time her croaking voice whispered in my ear, I felt as if she were putting a curse on me. My neck stiffened and goose bumps prickled my skin.

I was terrified she would discover that I was not, in fact, a good boy; that as soon as my grandmother saw that in my heart I despised her, she would become a demon, her white hair bristling and her eyes burning red, and she would devour me. I would break into a cold, heavy sweat, and some nights I found sleep impossible.

So I took great care that she wouldn't notice and showered her with adoration. I volunteered to bring her food and wipe the sweat from her brow. I cared for her diligently; I even went so far as to snuggle against her and kiss her cheek sweetly, telling her that I loved her.

Her cheek was dry as a withered leaf and smelled of the medicine I hated so much. Terrified that I might catch her disease, I would go to the sink afterward and scrub my mouth out with water over and over until finally I split my lip. As it bled, I considered what an awful child I was for lying; my throat clenched, and my eyes burned.

Then one day my grandmother grew cold and stopped moving.

"You are such a good boy, such a kind boy," she whispered, stroking my head tenderly.

Her hand went suddenly limp and her face turned white, the color of candle wax, but I felt nothing. When she stopped breathing, I deserted my grandmother and went to play in the park.

When I returned that evening, my mother caught me up in her arms and told me my grandmother had died, but even then, my heart was as placid as a forest where no animals ventured to go.

My grandmother's funeral was held a few days later. During all that time I was distant and shed not a single tear, so the adults murmured to each other, "He's still so young, he doesn't understand that his grandma is dead. He was so fond of her."

Shame welled up inside of me when I heard that. My ears burned red, and I couldn't meet anyone's eyes. But that was only embarrassment; I didn't feel the slightest bit sad at my grandmother's death.

I've been this way ever since I was very small.

How do you even write love letters?

I was in class the next day, struggling with my very first love letter, which I was drafting on a sheet of lined paper tucked under my notebook, feeling totally uninspired.

Dear Shuji Kataoka,

I apologize for writing you out of the blue.
You must have been very surprised.
My name is Chia Takeda, and I started my first year at Seijoh Academy this spring.
My name means "lots of love."
I saw you shooting with the archery team after school, and I thought you were great. I developed feelings for you.

Hmm . . . That sounds really formal.

Dear Shuji,

Hi! This is my first letter like this EVER!
My name's Chia Takeda, first-year class two, seat number twelve. I'm a Cancer, and my blood type is B.
Some of my friends call me Chee.
I know this is really sudden, but I love you!
Oh gosh, I'm so embarrassed!

I'm actually embarrassed to read this. And it makes her sound so stupid.

Blushing, I wrote letter after letter.

Why was I even doing this?

Tohko had kept mouthing off: "Your writing needs more sex appeal, so this is a great opportunity. I want you to learn from it. Put yourself inside little Chia's mind and write the syrupy, unpracticed confession of a love-struck girl. The world is still bright and shining, and you're just so *happy!* Something like that. Something that will impress the boy she gives it to and make him think, 'Whoa, she's so adorable,' and 'What an angelic heart to be so loved by.' "

Unbelievable. Tohko should have just written it herself.

"I focus on the eating," she would have said, giggling without a hint of shame.

A DNA helix was drawn on the blackboard, and the white-haired biology teacher was droning on about chromosomes, heritability, and whatever else as if reciting a liturgy.

Seijoh Academy was a serious school that students had to test into, so everyone was feverishly taking notes, contributing the scratching of pencils on paper to the teacher's recitation. Still, there were a couple kids playing with their cell phones under their desks, too.

I bet no one else is composing love letters, though. After all, love letters are passé; it's all about text messaging now.

Freshly reminded of the fact that I was writing love letters in class, color seeped across my face until it was totally red.

But these aren't my love letters. They're for Takeda. It's Takeda saying she likes Shuji, not me, and…wait, who am I justifying this to?

Besides, Tohko told me to do it. She said I should try putting myself inside Takeda's mind when I write.

I remembered Takeda's face as she joyously described the boy she liked to us, her cheeks flushed

"I like this boy named Shuji Kataoka. He's a third-year student

on the archery team! I was checking out a bunch of different clubs right after I started here, and then I saw Shuji practicing with the archery team. He drew his bow back *so* far, it was amazing, and then his face got this super-serious look, and he turned toward the target. The air felt as tense as the bow—and me, too. My eyes were glued on him. I stopped in my tracks and held my breath, seriously.

"Actually, I'd been feeling kind of down before that.

"But as soon as I saw Shuji looking at the target, that all disappeared from my mind, and when his arrow *twangggged* into the bull's-eye, I felt like it had shot into my heart, too.

"And then Shuji got this gentle look on his face, and he grinned just like a little kid. It was the most amazing smile of all the smiles I've ever seen! That's when I got my crush on him.

"I'm awful at sports, so I didn't join the archery team, but I went sometimes to their practice to watch Shuji. I heard the other members call him Kataoka and Shu and stuff, so that's how I found out his name. Shuji is usually a really cheerful guy, which he doesn't look like at all, and he jokes around constantly and makes everyone laugh.

"But when he's shooting an arrow, he gets superserious. Even though he might have been joking and laughing right before that, he gets this almost scary tension on his face, and it's only when he's drawing a bow...But then if he misses the target, he'll make a joke about it, and if he hits it, he shouts and celebrates it like a little kid, cheering and jumping around.

"I started wondering what Shuji thinks about when he's shooting arrows and then my mind just gradually filled up with him, and I wanted to know more about him, and I wanted him to know about me, too."

Takeda had gone on long enough to rival Tohko whenever she expounded on the fine points of a book. Her plump cheeks tinged

pink, her eyes flashing vivaciously, she talked us deaf about Shuji and looked truly overjoyed doing it.

So, you know. At the very least, I had to convey just how much Takeda liked Shuji. If Takeda was rejected because of my letter, I wouldn't be able to live with myself...

I flipped to a fresh sheet of paper and began writing out Takeda's feelings, line by line.

> I want you to know about me, Shuji.
> And I want to know lots more about you.
> So I decided to be brave and write you a letter.

"Here you go."

After classes ended for the day, I handed Takeda her letter.

"I threw this together during lunch. I didn't bother with a draft, so I can't guarantee it's any good..."

"Oh my gosh, thank you!"

Takeda bounced happily and accepted it.

"Oh wow, three whole pages? You wrote all this at *lunch?* I guess I shouldn't be surprised—you *are* the book club's top writer!"

"Uh, it's not *that* great..."

"Can I read it?" She giggled.

She started to unfold the paper and I rushed to stop her. "Ack! No! You can't read it here!"

"Aw, why not? I want to see it, too. You put your heart into writing that letter!"

Tohko smiled teasingly and tried to steal a peek at the letter over Takeda's shoulder.

I cut in between them. "No! Absolutely not!"

"Umm, I guess I'll go then. I need to hurry home and rewrite the letter. I have a stationery set all ready and everything! It's light pink with cherry petals falling across it. It's superadorable."

"Good idea."

I waved Takeda off in a haze.

"Bye! Good luck!"

"Thank you guys so much!"

"Don't forget your report!"

"I won't!" Takeda replied cheerily and waved to us, the letter clutched in her hand.

Halfway out, she toppled over, but she got right back up again and left, laughing in embarrassment. I watched her go, my heart pounding.

"Man, I really wanted to read that love letter, Konoha! You spent three whole days on it!"

I glanced over at Tohko, who sat on the fold-up chair hugging her knees, her bright eyes crinkling, and my ears burned with embarrassment. This was bad—she'd seen right through me.

I responded with deliberate sarcasm. "No way. If I gave it to you, you'd want to taste it and end up eating the whole thing."

Tohko stuck out her lip. "Come on, I'm not *that* crazy for food."

Then she laid her cheek on her knees and got a dreamy expression on her face. Her long, thin braids spilled over her frail shoulders like two cats' tails.

"A love letter would have been great, though. They must be all sweet and tickly and taste like happiness. Konoha, what do you think the most delicious story in the world is?"

"I dunno."

Tohko smiled. "I think it's a love letter the person you like poured his or her heart into writing for you. I mean, that would be the only copy in the world, a precious treasure that was just for you."

Her face turned sweetly shy as soon as she said that.

"Oh, but then it would be way too precious to ever eat. Wow,

24

I don't know what I would do. How could you have the best food in the world right in front of you and not be able to eat it?"

She touched a finger to her temple and looked seriously conflicted. I thought it was so funny, I burst out laughing.

"Oh, you know you would eat it! I'll bet you the collected works of Natsume Soseki you wouldn't have the letter a full night before the whole thing was in your belly."

"That's so mean! Really awful! You really are the one with no delicacy!" Tohko whined, spinning around in her chair to turn her back on me. She didn't forgive me until after I'd written her snack for her.

"I'll show you! I'm gonna write your name down a million times, then I'm gonna tear it up into tiny pieces and gobble up every single one. Then you'll be cursed!"

"Geez, you are so immature, Tohko."

At lunch the next day, Takeda came skipping to my classroom and chimed, "Excuse meee, is Konoha here?"

The class was instantly abuzz. I stood up quickly.

"Oh, there you are!"

Takeda waved at me. And oh man, the *stares*.

"Uh, come with me."

"Huh? Uh, all right."

I practically ran into the hall and around a corner and kept going until there was no one else around. When I asked her what she wanted, she looked up at me, a grin splitting her face.

"I waited for Shuji outside school this morning, and I gave him that letter you wrote for me."

"Really!"

She's *quick*. I tended to be listless, if anything, so her energy levels really impressed me.

"My heart was beating so fast! *Bump-bump, bump-bump!* I

gave the letter to Shuji and asked him to read it, then I made a break for it. I didn't hear a word my friends or the teachers said after that. All I could think about over and over was, 'I wonder if Shuji read my letter! I wonder what he thought!'"

"Th-then what happened?" I was practically on the edge of my seat.

"I couldn't think about anything else and I could barely eat my lunch, so I went to the archery practice hall. And Shuji was there, and—"

"Whoa! And then what?"

Takeda flushed with happiness and threw out a peace sign.

"He thanked me for the letter and said he really appreciated it! He said it was too sudden to be girlfriend-boyfriend right away and we should start slow."

"That's great!"

I felt like I could jump for joy right along with Takeda.

"Yeah! Shuji said he's never gotten such a cute letter before and it made him really happy. This is all thanks to you, Konoha. You really deserved to win the Adatara Literature of Love competition!"

"Ahaha...all I did was throw something together at lunch, really."

"No, I mean it! I think that letter really cheered Shuji up. So I promised I would write him letters every day from now on."

"What?" I asked stupidly.

Every day...?

Takeda grabbed my hands, and when she spoke, her voice was bubbling over with trust and reverence. "I know you can handle it, Konoha! You can just throw something together at lunch."

Starting the next day, Takeda would run to my class as soon as first period was over.

"Good morning, Konoha! Your letter was a huge hit with Shuji

26

yesterday! You really are amazing. You're a genius. I bet you wind up being an author!"

"Ha…um, you're too kind. Here's the one for today."

"Oh wow, thank you! I'll copy it in math class next period. I hope it makes Shuji happy."

"Yeah…"

My smile was a little strained.

Tohko giggled and informed me, "You had it coming. Now there's no choice but to stick with little Chia to the very end. Right, Mister Distinguished Author?"

She was straddling the fold-up chair, a paperback in one hand, looking up at me crookedly with her clear, teasing black eyes.

The book was *The Great Gatsby,* by F. Scott Fitzgerald.

"But you were the one who forced me to work with Takeda in the first place. And you were the one who set up some weird mailbox in the school courtyard without permission, too."

"I didn't force you, I *recommended* you. I said you would write wonderful love letters for her and listen to her seriously. Besides…" Tohko flopped her thin body forward and the chair screeched. Her pink lips cracked into a smile. "I wasn't the one who told her you wrote the letter in your spare time. That was you."

"Urk."

Tohko closed her eyes rapturously. "Oh, I hope little Chia's romance goes well! I wonder what kind of report she'll write for me. Will it be like a fluffy strawberry shortcake smothered in whipped cream? Or will it taste like chocolate infused with a dash of orange liqueur? I wouldn't mind something like a mille-feuille with loads of custard packed into crispy pie crust, either.…"

She never thought about anything but her treats. Her fantasizing must have made her hungry because she tore a page from *The Great Gatsby* and started to crunch on it.

"Mmmm, so good. Fitzgerald has a really snazzy flavor. I feel as if flamboyance, glory, and passion are dancing a waltz in my mouth, like I'm eating glittering caviar with champagne at a party. When I bite into it, its delicate skin pops, and a fragrant liquid spills into my mouth. The main character Gatsby is *so* innocent, I can't stop rooting for him."

Wasn't that story about Gatsby getting jerked around heartlessly by Daisy, his former lover and another man's wife, until it destroyed him? I wouldn't call that "snazzy." More like running over with pathos. But I suppose everyone interprets literature differently.

"Oh no!"

Tohko suddenly cried out as if the world were coming to an end. She twisted her face into a frown, her forehead crinkling.

"This is *awful!* I borrowed this book from the library, and I just accidentally *ate* it!"

I went to the library with Tohko to apologize for "accidentally dropping the book and it just *ripped!*" (Tohko said she was too scared to go alone and forced me to go with her). The day after, Takeda came to my class just as she always did.

"You making any progress with Shuji? Has he suggested going out or anything yet?"

We'd gone into the hall and stood there talking.

"Oh gosh, thank you for worrying about me! You're sooo nice, Konoha. I'm touched!"

I blushed. I was just sick of writing letters and wanted them to hurry up and get together already.

"Actually, thanks to your letters I've gotten tons closer to Shuji, so I'm thinking maybe just one more little push..."

"You have to keep ramping things up like that," I said with conviction. Takeda nodded, rapt.

"Okay! I'm gonna take it to the limit! I've been keeping notes for my report, you know. Look!"

She gleefully held up the notebook she'd been hugging to her chest. It was about half the size of a school notebook, and it had a picture of a yellow duck on the cover. Takeda had sworn she was an awful writer, but she was sure gung-ho about it.

"It's a little embarrassing, but it's actually so much fun writing about someone I like. Oh, but I'd feel so dumb showing you my notes. I wrote such lame stuff. I have to reread them and make a clean copy."

"If that's how you feel, maybe you should try writing the letters yourself?"

Takeda hid behind her notebook and shook her head fiercely.

"Oh, I couldn't do that! I'd be so embarrassed! But you're right. I'd like to write for Shuji myself eventually. But until then, Mister Inoue, I know I can count on you!"

Sigh. I would have to keep ghostwriting these things after all.

Just then Takeda looked at me uneasily.

Cheeks flushed, peering over the edge of her notebook and looking completely unsure of herself, she hesitantly asked, "Um...do you think I'm annoying?"

I jumped. "What? N-no, not at all! I think it's kind of fun writing these love letters, too. Ha-ha!"

Before I could stop myself, I'd told an outright lie.

But Takeda smiled innocently at it, like a little puppy. "Great! I can't wait to see tomorrow's letter!"

She'd cheered up instantaneously and, waving her hand instead of the tail she lacked, she ran off, looking like she might tumble over at any moment.

Sigh...I'm such a fraud.

When I went back to class, shoulders slumped, the boys started teasing me. "Your girlfriend is over here every day," and "Way to

go, scoring one of the new girls so fast! I didn't think you were the type."

"Geez, guys, it's not like that," I retorted weakly, laughing.

I didn't want to draw people's attention or hear their reactions. I was done exposing myself to unnecessary risks by standing out. If heaven dropped an extravagant gift into my lap, I wasn't strong or shameless enough to act like I deserved it.

As I was sitting down, I felt someone's eyes on me. I turned around and saw a girl staring at me.

Nanase Kotobuki.

She had bleached brown hair and a knockout figure. She was one of the girls in our class whom everyone noticed because of her flashy, cosmopolitan style and her tendency to say exactly what she thought.

Boys were always gossiping about her. "Kotobuki's so harsh, but I'd still go out with her."

I was under the impression that she hated me. That's because ever since classes had started in April, she would sometimes grace me with this same frosty look.

I don't remember doing anything to deserve the glares, though. Oh wait, maybe yesterday...

I was zoned out when Kotobuki came toward me with a haughty expression pasted on her face, stuck her hand out at me, and brusquely demanded, "Four hundred and sixty yen."

"Wha—?"

"That's how much it's going to cost to replace the book you dropped that 'just ripped' yesterday. We collect fines for books that are lost or damaged."

"Hey, hold on! Yesterday you told us not to worry about it!"

When I'd gone to the library yesterday with Tohko to apologize, Kotobuki had been the one at the desk.

I'd thought to myself, *Ack, why did it have to be Kotobuki's shift?*

31

I'd prepared myself to get put through the wringer, but despite her severe expression, she released us without a fight. "You didn't do it on purpose. Try to be more careful next time."

So why this thing with the 460 yen? And why ask me? Tohko was the one who'd ripped (or rather, eaten) the book.

Kotobuki's eyebrows hiked dangerously higher.

"I can't exactly send Amano a bill. She pulls a lot of weight at the library. She can find books better than the librarians. Plus a lot of the student aides owe her favors. When I was a first-year student and didn't know where a book went, she helped me out, too. So you have to pay for her, Inoue."

"Um, Kotobuki... don't you think that's a little unorthodox?"

"Not at all," she replied crisply.

Man, and she didn't hesitate at *all* when she said that. I didn't want things to escalate, so I got out my wallet and placed a five-hundred-yen coin in her hand with a deep bow.

"I sincerely apologize for any trouble my club's president may have caused."

Closing her fist around the coin, Kotobuki frowned. "I'll give you your change later. If you tell Amano, I'll hit you."

Geez, how come I had to clean up Tohko's messes?

I'd expected Kotobuki to be done with me, but she still didn't go away. Instead, she just kept glaring at me.

"So that first-year student who keeps coming to see you all the time... is she your girlfriend?"

"You mean Takeda? No, we're not going out."

"Oh really? She works at the library, so I know a little bit about her. She strikes me as clumsy but totally natural, and it seems like she could be the victim of some guy's Lolita fantasy pretty easily. Are you *sure* you're not dating?"

Victim of a Lolita fantasy? What a horrible thing to say. But

since arguing would just encourage her, I smiled instead. "I'm just helping Takeda out, since Tohko asked me to."

Kotobuki's eyebrows went up even farther and a look of rage came over her face.

Er...did I mess that up somehow?

Kotobuki sucked in a breath, then frigidly replied, "I don't actually care who you're dating. But if you're not going out, you should lay off the lovey-dovey meet-ups in the hallway. It's pathetic how blatant you're being."

She let loose what venom she had, then left.

I had history class next. While I was copying the notes on the blackboard, I thought about how badly I needed to shove Takeda off on Shuji, and fast.

I was still thinking about all the harsh things Kotobuki had dumped on me, after all.

How was I going to get out of this? Maybe I should stand up for myself and write a letter full of real passion....

The clear sky had clouded over, and drops of water began to spatter the window.

It's raining...I wonder if I left an umbrella in the club locker.

⇒•◇•⇐

As I grew older, my impression that there was a significant disconnect between the way that I and other people experienced things grew only stronger. It took all the energy I had to summon even the slightest sympathy for things that made other people happy or sad.

Why does that make them happy?

Why does that make them sad?

When everyone was excited, cheering for their friends in

sports competitions, when they were depressed at losing a friend who transferred to another school, I felt as uncomfortable as if I were in a room full of foreigners with whom I shared no common language. I flinched away from them and felt sharp pains in my stomach. The crushing din of words that everyone spoke around me was utterly incomprehensible to me.

One day, someone stuffed firecrackers into the mouth of our class rabbit, and it died a horrible death. While everyone else was sobbing, I felt ill at ease and stared at my fingers and tried to make myself very small.

Why? Because I didn't feel the least bit sad about the rabbit's death.

I remembered how charming the rabbit had been in life, and its soft fur. But try as I might to feel sad, my heart remained unmoved, and I was unable to shed so much as a single tear. Stealing a glance at the others, I saw that I was the only one not crying.

That made my neck flush bright red, a feeling of such shame and terror that my ears roared with pounding blood.

Why? Why were they all crying? I just couldn't understand it. But it would be odd for one person to be unperturbed while the rest of them wept. I had to act like I was crying. My face was tense, so I couldn't cry very convincingly. My cheeks burned. What would I do if someone realized I was faking my tears? I just wouldn't lift my face. Hang your head and look upset. Ah, and now everyone's guffawing. I wonder what's so funny. I have no idea. But if I don't do the same as everyone else, they'll think I'm strange and cast me out.

Laugh. Laugh. Laugh. No, cry. Cry. No, laugh, you have to laugh.

If I can't do such a simple thing, I *am* strange, a freak.

My stomach twisted itself into knots with the shame and fear I felt at being unable to share everyone else's emotions. I imagined the cold stares they would give me when I was exposed.

I'm like the one black sheep born into a pure white flock.

Unable to enjoy the things my peers enjoyed, unable to grieve the things they grieved, unable to eat the things they ate—being born an ignoble black sheep, I didn't understand the things my friends found pleasant, such as love, kindness, and sympathy. I simply dusted my dark wool in white powder and pretended I was a white sheep, too.

If my peers discovered that I was in fact a black sheep, they would gang up on me and stab me with their horns and trample me with their hooves. Please, please, don't find out, don't find out.

Each time the rain fell, each time the wind blew, I shuddered in anticipation of the white powder I'd used to cover myself falling off, of someone shouting, "Hey, he's a black sheep!" and I had not a moment of ease in my heart. But there was nothing else I could do.

I did my best to smile pleasantly at my parents, my teachers, my classmates; I became a mime to make them laugh. Oh please, don't notice that I'm a monster who doesn't understand human emotion. I'll pretend to be a person so stupid they redefine idiocy, and while everyone is laughing at me and pitying me and forgiving me, please let me live on.

I'm still wearing my mask, still acting in this farce.

———◆———

"Wow, it's really coming down!"
I was walking down a dimly lit hallway after school.

35

It wasn't really that late yet, but outside the window it was dark and the sky was heavy with black clouds. Fat drops of rain stabbed at the earth, chilling the air with the sound of their impact.

The air was brisk and humid.

"The chance of rain was only supposed to be fifty percent today, too. Man…"

It would have been fine if my umbrella had still been in the book club's locker.

But when I opened the locker, I discovered that the umbrella I'd put in there when it rained last week was gone.

"Oh, sorry! I borrowed it the last time it rained and forgot to put it back," Tohko said casually.

That day, the two of us had run home together, getting soaked.

"You need to put things back when you're done with them!"

"I knowwww. But darting through the rain like this is so exhilarating. It feels so youthful!"

She thinks everything belongs to her, and no one better question it…

Not even Miss Piggy was as self-absorbed as she was. Seriously, why was I even in this club?

Hmm…it's a mystery.

I'd had cleaning duty today, but the time had gone by in a flash. I was surprised at how late it had gotten by the time I finished up the work my homeroom teacher had assigned. Tohko was probably clattering her chair around, wondering where her snack was. There were lots of old books in the club room, but they didn't keep very well in that environment and, as Tohko put it, "They're past their expiration dates. They would mess up my stomach."

"But you know," she added with a very serious face, "if they're stored properly, I think old books must have the taste of an aged wine or truffle. It makes me drool just thinking about it. And then, you know what else? Those handwritten manuscripts of Soseki and Ōgai and Mushanokoji that are on display at their memorial museums—I bet those taste better than anything you can *imagine!* I wouldn't even care if they messed with my stomach. I wonder if I'll ever get a taste."

I was seriously concerned that Tohko might someday try to break into one of those museums.

As I was climbing the stairs to the book club room, I halted. "Oh man, I forgot my classics textbook."

The classics teacher was really strict, and since I had the class tomorrow, I'd intended to review at home tonight.

I decided to go all the way back to the classroom to get it.

The halls were almost deserted, probably because of the rain, and very quiet.

I was reaching out to open the classroom door when I heard voices inside. Apparently some girls were still here talking.

I was reluctant to barge into a group of girls alone, and while I hung back in the hallway, I picked up the sound of their conversation.

"What! Eri, you're after Akutagawa, too? *Seriously?*"

"Urf, you like him, too? That means we're rivals, Mori."

"Hang on! I think Akutagawa is hot, too."

"No *way!* That makes three of us, Micks!"

Apparently they were talking about the boys they liked.

And they weren't talking about Akutagawa, the famous author, but the tallest, most taciturn guy in our class. He looked very mature, his features sort of cool and insightful, so I could see why he was so popular.

But now what was I gonna do? It just got way harder to go in there.

"Awesome! It's me and Hirosaki forever, then! No competition for me!"

"Oh, so you like Hirosaki, huh, Suzuno?"

"You know it. I've got a thing for bad boys. And as a matter of fact, we're going to go see the dolphins next Saturday!"

"*What?*"

"When did *that* happen?"

"It's only been a month since we got our new classes! You move way too fast!"

"I haven't said more than 'good morning' and 'see you' to Akutagawa yet. You're treating me to a Häagen-Dazs, Suzuno!"

"Me, too! Two scoops, too, not just one!"

"Oh man, that's going to be tough to do after I buy all the clothes for my date. How about some ice cream cups instead?"

The girls laughed, joking and playing together.

Hmmm. Maybe it would be better to go to the club room and just come back later.

"Okay, now it's Nanase's turn."

"Yeah! Everyone else fessed up, so now you've got to come clean, too."

Nanase—as in Kotobuki? So she was in there, too.

"I know you don't like Akutagawa, too."

"Don't even *say* that! She's superhot, I could never compete."

"I..."

I heard Kotobuki's voice through the door.

I knew I shouldn't be listening, but I wanted to know what kind of person a rude, uncompromising girl like her would go for. I held my breath.

"I don't like anyone. There is someone I hate, though."

"Oo, who?"

"Konoha Inoue."

Kotobuki said my name with perfect clarity.

My thoughts ground to a momentary halt then. The next moment, my brain burned with fury.

"What? Why? He's so nice, how can anyone hate him?"

"Seriously. He's so harmless and ethereal, don't you think?"

"He's got a boring personality so he doesn't really stand out, but if you look real, *real* hard, he's cute."

"Yeah! And he's so nice to talk to, and he's always smiling. What's wrong with that?"

Kotobuki answered in an irritated tone. "That's what's so infuriating. He's always got this deliberate little smile on his face. You never know what he's actually thinking. It's creepy."

Heat seeped slowly out from my cheeks all the way to my ears, and my hands shook. My throat felt tight.

Why did she have to say stuff like that about me? I mean, I knew she hated me, but this... Talking about me so spitefully in front of all those people...

My sliver of pride fought down my desire to flee, and I put a hand to the classroom door. I shoved it aside, and the girls turned in unison to look at me.

I gaped at them, pretending I hadn't heard anything. "Oh, hey, you're all still here. Hope I'm not interrupting."

The girls looked away uncomfortably. I went straight to my desk and grabbed my textbook.

"Can you believe I forgot my book? We have the class tomorrow and everything!"

Kotobuki was glowering at me, her face flushed. I turned toward her and smiled for all I was worth.

"I'll see you, guys!"

The girls bade me a clumsy good-bye.

Kotobuki was the only one who kept her mouth firmly shut, instead continuing to sulk and glare at me.

That was awful. I'm so embarrassed.

I walked down the damp, unlit hallway feeling small and close to breaking.

What does she mean, "a deliberate little smile"? "It's creepy"?

There were times when it was better to shut up and smile in order to smooth things over, rather than trying to get your own way by clashing with everyone around you or destroying the mood somewhere by giving voice to your unfiltered feelings.

Times when that was all you could do.

And still she called me infuriating.

Not like I'm crazy in love with her, either.

A scream rose up at the back of my throat, along with a lump of heat.

It was different before. Before I...

"Konoha, you look so happy when you smile."

"And you're SO easy to read. Whenever you're depressed or annoyed or scrambling to get something done, it pops right onto your face. You're just like a puppy."

If I argued that it was mean of her to call me a dog, she would just giggle, her voice a tinkling bell.

"Look, you're sticking your lip out again. You are way too easy to read. But I like that about you, Konoha. I can relax when I'm with you."

When I was in middle school, there was a girl I liked, too. I was in love, just like everybody else.

Just hearing her voice made my heart beat faster. I treated every word she spoke to me as though it were a special treasure, and locked it away in my heart. Before I went to sleep each night, I would take them out and gaze at them, one after another.

That small happiness filled my days. I was always smiling.

But my love, like the Great Gatsby's, ended in tragedy, and I learned how to lie.

⟫◈⟪

My effort paid off and my "human" act began to be pretty convincing.

The people I know say I'm fun and cheerful and kind.

It was a relief to be degraded and laughed at, but when people told me I was kind, I felt uncomfortable, as if my stomach were convulsing.

I wanted people to think I was good, and so I made babies laugh with a funny face and played with dogs. But when I did those things, my cheeks burned with shame.

Because all of it was a lie. Because I was, in fact, not a kind person in any way. Because I was scamming them.

So every time someone said I was kind, I was overcome by an impulse to cry out, to tear my stomach open and kill myself.

Ignorant of this turmoil inside me, dogs would joyfully wag their tails and trot after me when I patted them on the head. They must have believed I was a kind person.

The girl who told me that she liked me was a little like a dog.

Innocent and cheerful, always laughing brightly. She was very childlike.

How wonderful it would have been to be like that, too.

But part of me hated that peaceful, simple girl.

Tohko had her stockinged feet propped up on a folding chair, turning through the pages of a book as she listened to the rain falling.

Today's meal was a magnificent hardcover edition of *The Iliad*, the epic poem by the blind poet Homer chronicling the Trojan War.

Her black braids poured over her shoulders down to her waist like cats' tails, her long, perfect eyelashes casting a faint shadow over her eyes. One slender finger played with her lips—a habit Tohko had while reading. Sometimes she would nibble on her fingertip.

The dust-caked windowpane was wet with rain. There was no light from the setting sun today.

I stopped in the middle of my writing to ask, "Do you like anybody, Tohko?"

"Hm? What did you say?"

When she was lost in a book, she didn't really register people talking to her.

"Oh, did you finish my snack already?"

Light broke out across her face. It was so typical of her to let her fixation on food interrupt her reading, despite how much she was focused on her book.

"I asked if there's anybody you like."

"Of course there is. Let's see, Gallico of course, and Dickens, and Dumas, oh and Stendahl, and Chekhov, and Shakespeare, and don't forget Olcott, and then there's Montgomery, and Farjeon and Lindgren and MacLachlan and Cartland and Jordan, and also Saikaku and Soseki and Ōgai, and Kenji Miyazawa and Yuichi Kimura, and, and, and..."

Tohko went on and on, looking as if she might start drooling at any moment, until I interrupted. "I'm not talking about food. And who are Cartland and Jordan? Basketball players?"

"You mean you don't know who Barbara Cartland and Penny Jordan are? They're both famous romance novel authors. Cartland's *The Key of Love* is essential reading. It's about the daughter of an American oil baron who hides her identity and falls in love with a rich, handsome man.

"And Jordan's *Silver* was even made into a comic book. It was a huge hit. I definitely recommend that one, too. The shock of being betrayed by the man she loves turns innocent Geraldine's hair silver. She decides to get revenge on the evil man, and in order to make him her prisoner, she starts taking *super*intense lessons in seduction from a handsome tutor. The tutor is a sexy, wonderful guy."

We were getting further and further off track here...

"Okay, that's enough. I get it. Tohko, what I meant was...have you ever been in love?"

"Huh?" Tohko cocked her head, bewildered. "In...Lovecraft?"

"No, not Lovecraft. Have you ever had feelings for someone? Not hunger, *feelings,* as in *love,* as in a relationship."

"In that case, I'm always in love."

"I told you I'm not talking about food. I'm asking if you've ever been in love with a *person*."

I felt tired. No matter how depressed I was, I'd been an idiot to think I could talk with this girl about romance.

Then I noticed Tohko smirk, a distant look flashing in her eye.

Huh? Where had this mature, serious aura come from? I could practically hear the strains of a noir theme playing in the background. Was it possible that Tohko's past contained a painful experience with love?

43

"Well, you see... I'm inside a zone of romantic slaughter."

"Uhhh, what? What's *that* supposed to be?"

I had steeled myself for anything, but a voice strained by incredulity escaped me nonetheless.

Tohko turned a nihilistic gaze to the rain-soaked window and began to tell her story in a matter-of-fact tone that was yet replete with sorrow.

"At the beginning of this year, I asked a lady in Shin—to tell my fortune in love. She told me that I'd been inside a zone of romantic slaughter ever since I was born, and even if I fell in love I would just be spinning my wheels and peril would crash down around me like a raging storm. Even if I were accepted, she said my love would be short-lived and would shatter into hundreds of itty-bitty pieces. So she told me to focus on my studies and hobbies and not even think about falling in love."

"You mean that lady who sits outside the I—tan department store, who's always got the big line? You waited to see *her?*"

"Yeah. Snow had dusted the city cold and white that day."

"Why would you go line up on a snowy day?"

"I thought it would be less crowded that way. It only took thirty minutes to get my turn."

I felt a headache creeping in.

"You wanted the lady in Shin—to tell your fortune that badly?"

"I *am* a girl, you know. I want to know what my fortunes in love will be, just like anyone else. But to find out I'm in a zone of romantic slaughter... that was hard to hear. Oh, but guess what! She said that the romantic slaughter would end in seven years and then I would meet the man of my destiny!"

Pensive Tohko disappeared in a flash of cheer that filled her face. She leaned forward eagerly.

"She predicted that seven years from now, in the summertime, I would meet a man wearing a white scarf and standing in front of a bear with a salmon in its mouth, and we would fall into a fated love. And she made sure I understood that my love line was shockingly short and that this would be my first and only chance at love, so I had to be sure to make something of it. So unfortunately, I've sworn off love for the next seven years."

"But why would that guy be wearing a scarf in the summer? And if you try flirting innocently in front of a bear, you're going to get eaten."

Tohko pouted. "You've got no imagination, Konoha."

"You've got too much."

"Well, I *am* a book girl."

"You can't just wave everything away with that excuse. But you know, never mind. Sorry I interrupted your reading."

Tohko looked troubled. "Um...did something happen, Konoha?"

"No."

"Is there...someone you like?"

I looked away.

Rain tapped against the window.

"No, there isn't someone I like. It's nothing. That's the best..."

Nothing happening.

Not having a crush on anybody.

I could live in peace, without pain, or sadness, or disappointment.

I prayed that every day would be that way for the rest of my life.

I was never going to fall in love again.

Tohko looked at me in silence.

One year earlier, when she'd dragged me into the book club,

I had often made Tohko look sad. Every single time she made a face like that, I thought how unfair it was, considering what she was like. But still I'd be filled with embarrassed remorse.

"I'm going to go home. Sorry."

The silence was making me uncomfortable, so I got up, leaving my story half-written.

I opened the rusted locker and saw that the umbrella I'd left there was gone, just as I'd predicted.

"Here." Tohko held out a pale violet pocket umbrella with a cheerful smile. "I've still got your umbrella. You can use this one."

"What are you going to do, though?"

"Oh, I've *got* my umbrella. A really big one."

"...I see. Then thank you."

"Sure thing. See you tomorrow!"

She waved at me, her smile deliberately bright and untroubled.

I opened the umbrella when I stepped through the main entrance, making violets bloom in the gray rain with a *pop*.

Violet was Tohko's favorite color. I'd often seen her with handkerchiefs or pencils this same pale purple color.

"The rain doesn't look like it's going to let up..."

I stood where I was, holding the umbrella.

I'd known that Tohko was lying. She'd only had one umbrella.

Since starting high school, I'd put on a mask for my classmates and kept some distance between us. Even if I smiled, I wasn't really smiling. And I had felt small and pathetic when Kotobuki had pointed that out.

But for some reason I could act naturally with Tohko.

Every time I saw Tohko looking sad or troubled, I wished I could smile for her, even if it was fake. But I only managed some inept reassurance. I hated it.

How could I get better at lying?

Could I manage not to get hurt and to not hurt anyone else?

I don't know how long I stood there waiting for Tohko to come out, gazing up at the cold rain.

I saw a girl in a school uniform run out from behind the building.

Takeda.

She noticed me, too, and stopped.

She gasped and her eyes widened.

Then she whispered hoarsely, "Shuji?"

Huh?

The next moment, she was clinging to me and sobbing.

"What's wrong, Takeda?"

She didn't answer, only pressed her dripping face and body against me, circling her arms around my back and wailing. Tears streamed from her eyes, which she kept tightly shut as if in pain.

I was holding my bag and umbrella, so I couldn't hug her back. Besides, this was the first time this had ever happened to me, and I wasn't sure what I should do. Had something happened with her and Shuji? I was just about to ask when we heard a voice call out, "Chee!"

It was a boy about my age.

Takeda trembled against my chest when she heard him.

"Chee?"

The voice was coming closer, and from the same direction Takeda had come running from earlier. He sounded troubled somehow. Suddenly, Takeda pulled on my arm.

"T-Takeda, wait…"

Takeda set her jaw and tugged at my arm with a grim expression, pulling me away.

"Takeda, that guy is looking for you. Chee is you, isn't it?"

"No! Don't answer!"

She sounded terrified. She pulled me into the school building.

As we went in, I saw a boy carrying a navy blue umbrella go by, turning his head this way and that. But it was only a momentary glimpse, and I couldn't really see his face.

It wasn't until we reached the corridor to the back of the school yard that Takeda finally let go of my arm. She huddled into a ball and started to cry, her shoulders shaking.

—————◆—————

I told the girl that I would go out with her.

She smiled at me as naively as a puppy.

She had placed an innocent trust in me.

An uncorrupted, pure-hearted, gentle, happy white sheep beloved by God.

I envied her, was repelled by her, but at the same time I couldn't help but adore her simple effervescence.

But, perhaps, just such a girl might be able to change me.

They say that love changes people.

If so, that girl might be my salvation.

I might become a normal human being, rather than a monster possessing neither love nor kindness.

Oh, how I wish that I could.

I wished it so ardently that my heart seemed on fire.

Let me come to care for that girl.

Even if at first it's only an act, I know that eventually it would have to become true.

Please—please—let her innocent light deliver me.

But if that girl knew that I had killed someone, would she still love me? Would she still think that I was kind?

I am a monster.

That day, when tender flesh was pulverized and red blood spread its tangy aroma across the black asphalt, I watched with an empty heart.
I had killed a person.

Chapter 3 – The First Letter—Shuji Kataoka's Confession

Shuji.

That's what Takeda had called me.

She wouldn't tell me why she'd been crying so hard.

I waited until her tears stopped and then walked her home. As we walked through the rain together under Tohko's violet umbrella, Takeda kept her eyes down and said nothing. I had stolen a closer look and saw that her eyes were red from crying, and her lip was slightly swollen and tinged with blood. From time to time, she would glance up at me, wary and surreptitious, as if to reassure herself of something, and then would quickly look back down, blinking rapidly.

Finally we reached a two-story house with neatly tended flower beds, and we went our separate ways.

"Thank you so much for walking me home."

"No problem. You should go change out of those clothes and warm back up."

Takeda looked up at me again. She peered at my face as if she saw something written there, then looked back down with tears in her eyes. She ducked in a quick bow and disappeared behind her door.

We were in the first-period break the next morning, and she hadn't come. I stayed in my seat, constantly glancing over at the door, so when she came into the classroom, my eyes met Kotobuki's.

Ack, now what?

She looked flustered, too, and though I didn't move a muscle, she walked over to stand in front of me, her lips pressed thin and tight.

"Here's your change."

She stuck a fist out at me brusquely.

"Oh, thanks.... Uh, this is fifty yen."

Kotobuki had dropped a fifty-yen coin into my hand.

"Isn't this ten yen too much?"

"I know that. Give me change for my change."

"Um, sorry, I don't have any small change right now."

"Later is fine," she muttered irritably. She was fidgeting, apparently reluctant to go away just yet. "Chia Takeda's not coming today, huh?"

"Uh, yeah. I guess not."

"So yesterday after school...you came back in here all of a sudden, remember? Are you *sure* you didn't hear anything?"

She peered at me.

I smiled easily. "Was there something I should have heard?"

Kotobuki's face flushed an impressive shade of red. "I-if you didn't hear anything, then never mind."

She turned her back on me and returned to her desk.

I still had the fifty-yen coin in my hand.

The chime announcing second period rang out gently overhead.

Takeda didn't come...

She didn't appear during the second break, either.

I started to worry that she'd caught a cold and stayed home,

and I decided to go see how she was. While I hesitated outside Takeda's classroom, she came through the door herself, laughing with a group of friends.

"Geez, I can't believe you! You're awesome, Yoyo! Fine—I'm gonna bake a cake for his birthday and put my whole heart into it! Oh—"

Takeda had just struck a heroic pose when she saw me. Her eyes widened and she dropped her hands. "Konoha..."

"Uh, morning."

"Oh my God, what're you doing here? Oh, sorry, Yoyo, you go ahead. Konoha, come with me?"

Takeda took hold of my arm and started walking down the hallway. She was practically skipping.

What the heck? Why is she so cheerful? I was so confused.

Takeda brought me to a deserted spot in the hall, then turned around with a smile.

"Heh-heh-heh...what a surprise to have you come to me, Konoha."

"I was just wondering if you were all right...since you were crying yesterday."

"Oh, that? It wasn't anything important, really. I guess I just got a little high-strung or something. I guess I was a little down because of the rain. And you looked at me so kindly...I guess I just got carried away with it. Oh geez, it's so embarrassing. Please just forget that happened."

She flapped her hands back and forth, her face bright red. She was acting so much like she always did that I started to wonder if I had just imagined her tortured sobbing yesterday.

"Nothing happened with you and Shuji?"

Was that boy who'd come looking for her Shuji? He'd called her "Chee," as if he knew her really well.

Takeda's expression clouded over suddenly.

So something *had* happened.

"It's just…it seems like something is bothering him. He gave me a letter yesterday, but the things it said…"

A letter?

"Oh! But I'm totally fine! Really!"

Her hand popped back up and she struck her heroic pose again.

"Oh yeah! Can I have another letter today, Konoha?"

"Sure. I brought it with me."

When I handed her the folded paper, her face dissolved into joy.

"Thank you so much! I'm sure once Shuji reads this he'll cheer up, too. Oh, I have to go—my next class is in a different room. Eek!"

Takeda's foot caught on something, and she tumbled to the ground. I quickly helped her up.

"Heh-heh…thank you. I'm such a klutz. Okay, see you!"

I watched her patter off haphazardly, unsure of my own thoughts.

Takeda had said that something was bothering Shuji.

Was her crying yesterday somehow related to that?

What kind of person was Shuji Kataoka, anyway? I'd written lots of letters addressed to him, but I only knew him through Takeda's stories.

He was a third-year student on the archery team, had lots of friends, and was good at making people laugh.

He was always upbeat and smiling. He only got serious when he was shooting arrows.

He'd seemed pretty nice, but when she talked to him, he turned out to be *super*nice.

All this was what Takeda had told me.

Maybe Shuji wasn't the kind of person Takeda thought he was. Love often clouds the judgment, so it was an easy scenario to imagine.

"You're on the archery team, right?"

During clean-up that day, I struck up a conversation with my classmate, Akutagawa.

"Yeah, I am," he answered matter-of-factly in his deep, grown-up voice as he moved desks around.

He wasn't angry; he just wasn't a talkative guy. I had never seen him guffaw. That detachment probably appealed to girls. Looking at him up close like this, he really was pretty cool with his height and his muscular arms and shoulders and his calmly handsome features. Unlike me.

"Do you guys have a third-year student named Shuji Kataoka on the team?"

Akutagawa looked as though he was thinking for a very brief moment, then replied curtly, "Don't know him."

"Huh? Um, maybe his name is a little different. I heard that people call him Shushu or Shu or something like that."

"We've got a guy named Shuya Fujiwara, but he's second-year, not third. And I don't think anyone ever called him Shushu."

"Seriously? There's no one else named Shu-something?"

"Never heard of one."

What did this mean? Maybe Takeda had made a mistake. Well, that would have been possible before she'd told him how she felt, but now she was giving him letters and talking to him regularly. Was it really possible that she had his name wrong?

When Akutagawa had finished moving the desks, he looked at me.

"Do you have some problem with this Shu guy?"

"Uh, he's a friend of a friend, and—Oh hey! Do you think I could come watch you guys?"

"Sure. Sometimes new recruits come watch us practice."

"Could I come today?...Although, I'm not a recruit. Maybe it's not allowed?"

"Don't think anyone cares. I'll find out."

"Thanks, Akutagawa."

The archery team's practice hall was an old wooden building to one side of the gym. Five wooden targets were hung up on the far wall. They also had bales of straw on platforms secured from behind by wooden planks, old floorboards, and other stuff set up as targets.

The team members wore chest guards over traditional white uniforms and black pants. They pulled the bows into tight curves, then sent their arrows flying. Along the side, a few dozen kids wearing sweats were using thick rubber bows and arrows, swinging them around as they called out in unison, "Plant your feet!" "Square the chest!" "Raise the bow!" They were probably first-years.

Akutagawa came over to me, dressed in his practice clothes.

"I got you permission. It's dangerous, so don't get in anybody's way."

"I won't."

Just then the sound of an arrow striking one of the old floorboards shot through me.

"Wow, I didn't know it was that loud! It really is intimidating seeing it up close."

I remembered Takeda mentioning that. She'd said that the moment Shuji's arrow struck the target, it had lodged in her heart as well.

"I guess it can surprise you the first time you hear it, yeah,"

Akutagawa replied gruffly, then he left me behind to go join the practice.

I observed the team members from the back of the room.

The archery team practiced all together, both boys and girls, and the squad seemed about evenly split between them. There were a lot of people on the team; I counted fifty with a quick glance.

I expected Shuji, the boy Takeda had fallen in love with at first sight, to be among them.

Lessee...it was love at first sight, so he has to be pretty good-looking. So forget that guy. Not that guy, either. That guy over there isn't quite...

About halfway through, I wanted to pull out my hair.

This was bad. The number of candidates was decreasing steadily.

Akutagawa is definitely the best-looking guy on the archery team. But Takeda said Shuji is actually happy-go-lucky and popular, even if he doesn't look it. There's no way to spin Akutagawa as happy-go-lucky...But maybe he's only distant in class and he gets more upbeat with the team. Hmm...

In the end, I couldn't decide which of them might have been Shuji.

During a break in the practice, Akutagawa came over to me and whispered in his low, flat voice, "I asked the captain about people named Shuji, but he said he didn't know any."

The mystery only deepened.

Thanking Akutagawa, I left the archery team and headed to the book club.

"Choo!"

I heard a cute sneeze.

"Choo! Mmrf..."

Tohko pulled a tissue out of a box and blew her nose.

"Oh, hello, Konoha. Ah-choo!"

She sneezed again and demurely blew her nose.

The trash can at her feet was full of pink tissues.

So she'd gotten soaked on her way home yesterday, after all, and caught a cold.

"Uh, thank you for the umbrella yesterday."

I held the violet umbrella out to her awkwardly, and Tohko beamed at me with bleary eyes and a nose as red as a reindeer's.

"Yoooou're welcome! And I put your umbrella back in the locker. Sorry I kept it so long."

"You look like you have a cold. Are you okay?"

"I'm fine! I was rereading Cartland's *Theirs to Eternity* in the bath and lost track of time, so I didn't notice the water getting cold. I'll be all better soon."

"You shouldn't stay in the bath so long that the water gets cold. The pages of your book are going to get soggy and fall apart, you know."

"And *that* is *also* de-*li*-cious. Like dipping a biscuit in pink champagne, maybe?"

"I doubt that champagne tastes like cold bathwater or bubble bath."

"Geez, you have *no* imagination whatsoever, do you? Ah-choo!...*Hnk*...Anyway, you sure took your time getting here today, Konoha. Did you have clean-up duty again?"

"Um, no...I went to watch the archery team practice."

"*Hnk*...the archery team?"

Tohko cocked her head, the tissue still covering her face. Her long braids swung smoothly.

"Actually..."

I summarized how I'd run into Takeda yesterday after school, how she'd been crying, and how there was no one named Shuji Kataoka on the archery team.

"Oh my..."

Tohko was speechless.

Then, struck by an idea, she said, "Oh yeah! You should be able to search all the students' names on the computers in the library. Let's go see."

At the library, I saw that Kotobuki was behind the counter.

"Oh!"

As soon as she saw me, she glared, as if demanding to know what I was doing there.

"Could we use one of the computers?"

"There aren't that many patrons today, so one should be open."

"Thanks."

"Ah-choo! Don't mind us."

We slipped past the counter and headed to the computer corner. We found an open one and crowded together at it.

"Can you do it, Konoha? Machines and I don't get along."

Tohko sounded afraid.

"Don't get along? It's just a search."

I clicked the mouse to open Seijoh Academy's student roster and did a search for Shuji Kataoka. The hourglass icon appeared, then it showed a message saying there were no matches.

Next I did a search for just the name Shuji.

That had no matches, either.

There were seven hits for Kataoka, but four of them were girls and the three boys left didn't have first names even vaguely resembling "Shuji."

Tohko and I exchanged a look.

What was going on?

Shuji Kataoka was not only not a member of the archery team, but he wasn't even a student at our school.

The next day, Takeda appeared during the first-period break, clutching her duck notebook.

"Goooood moooorning! I came for my letter!"

Ignoring a look from Kotobuki, I led Takeda into a corner of the hallway.

"I don't have a letter today."

"Huh? Why not?"

"Because there's no such person as Shuji Kataoka at our school."

"Whaaat?" Takeda's eyes widened. It didn't look like an act—she seemed truly surprised. Then she started to giggle, as if I were telling a joke. "Come on, that's not true, Konoha. Shuji does too exist!"

"But there's no one on the archery team with that name and no one in the student rolls for the whole school. Who have you been giving your letters to, Takeda?"

Takeda's smile never faltered as she answered. "To Shuji!"

She showed not the slightest doubt, and I started to wonder if maybe I was the one who'd been mistaken.

"And Shuji is *too* on the archery team!"

"B-but—"

"I still have the letter he gave me, too! Look."

Takeda opened the duck notebook and took out the envelope stuck inside it. The envelope was plain white and showed no address; but the sender's name was there—Shuji Kataoka. Takeda pulled out the letter.

It was also on plain white paper, three folded sheets.

I remembered that yesterday Takeda had mentioned receiving a letter from Shuji. She'd started to tell me about it, but then her expression had darkened and she trailed off.

She'd also said that something seemed to be bothering him.

Had he written about that in this letter?

Takeda looked momentarily troubled, and she glanced up at me with that same wary look she sometimes had. Then she thrust the letter at me decisively.

"Shuji exists. Really. I'm sure of it. Read this letter and you'll see. He's suffering a lot right now...but I'm too dumb to understand what he means...so...so...please help him."

She appealed to me earnestly, her voice shaking. She may have acted cheerful, but she must have been reaching her limit, carrying this burden all alone. Takeda may have been hoping for salvation herself. I supposed that was why her gaze looked so helpless.

I knew that reading the letter would only mean more trouble for me.

If I read the letter, it would be a promise to help her.

A peaceful life without surprises was my greatest desire.

It was stupid to get involved in other people's business, especially when I had a choice about it. The best decision would be to tell her, *Sorry, I have enough to worry about already, and I don't think I can help anyway,* and then withdraw.

But it was too late for that. I was dying to find out whether this Shuji Kataoka person truly existed and discover how this misunderstanding had happened.

I unfolded the letter. I felt my fingertips tingle and I detected a tangy smell.

Mine has been a life of shame.
Human beings are inscrutable to me.

60

They, and their emotions—kindness, fondness, sadness—
which every one of them naturally possesses.

I donned the mask of a mime. I struggled to make them
laugh, to make them believe I was harmless. But with each
lie built atop lies, my spirit only depleted.

I killed someone that day.
When tender flesh was pulverized and red blood spread
its tangy aroma across the black asphalt, I watched with a
thirsty heart.
I had killed a person.
I doubt that God will ever forgive me.

"That's *No Longer Human*," Tohko declared upon finishing the
letter. We were in the club room after school.
"You mean the novel by Osamu Dazai?"
"Yeah. 'Mine has been a life of shame': that's a quote of the
opening line. There's a bunch of other lines that refer back to *No
Longer Human*, too."
She said all that and then sneezed once.
She appeared to have mostly recovered after a night's sleep, but
she still seemed a little foggy. Her eyes were still bleary.
"Then the stuff in this letter isn't true—it's just a parody of *No
Longer Human*?"
I hoped that was true. When I'd read the letter, the monstros-
ity and hopelessness of it made me feel as if an evil shadow had
fallen over me.
It was a stunning revelation—and a confession—by the young
Shuji Kataoka.
Ever since infancy, Shuji had been unable to share in the emo-
tions of others.

61

Why do they like that?

Why do they hate that?

What did it mean to "like" something, anyway? What did it mean to "hate" something?

Someone he was close to passed away, and everyone cried at the funeral. But he didn't feel sad at all. A friend transferred to a school far away. Everyone was sad he was leaving, but it didn't move his heart in the slightest. Shuji also couldn't understand why everyone fawned over babies and puppies. As these things continued to happen, he began to think of himself as inhuman, an unholy monster.

He couldn't understand things about people that he ought to have understood, and it made him afraid. Disappointed. Heartbroken.

What would people think if they found out he was a monster?

That fear made him take on the role of the clown and struggle to make people laugh and love him.

People were charmed by Shuji and he grew to be popular, but he always cherished an intense shame in his heart with which he continued to struggle.

He was ashamed of lying. Ashamed that he wasn't human. Shuji Kataoka stated that again and again in his letters.

I'm ashamed.

Ashamed.

Ashamed to be alive.

There was only one person who realized that Shuji's clowning was an act.

Shuji referred to that person as "S" and noted that although S understood him, they were also capable of destroying him—and were therefore dangerous.

Only one person, only S with that insightful gaze, has noticed my clowning.

When will I face destruction at S's hands?

S asked me once whether I truly loved her with all my heart.

The letter ended there.

It was impossible to tell who "her" referred to, or who S was. Or how Shuji responded to S's question.

When I finished the letter, I felt an unspeakable tightness in my chest. It was a feeling I'd experienced somewhere before. After Tohko's revelation, I remembered where.

It was the opening from *No Longer Human*.

It was Osamu Dazai's most famous work; I'd read it in middle school for a summer assignment. We had to pick one of four books and write an essay on our impressions of it. I had still wanted to push myself back then, so I picked the one that seemed hardest. My very first impression of it had been how dark the title was.

But I suppose I had been too immature to understand the protagonist's suffering. What I had taken away from it was that his morose confession had dragged on and on, and it was all jumbled up. In the end, I wrote my essay on a different book.

It was a long time ago, but apparently parts of what I read still lingered deep in my memory. When I'd read Shuji Kataoka's letter, I'd gotten the feeling that I had read something like it before.

"Ah-choo!"

Tohko sneezed.

"Mmrf…I wouldn't say the whole letter is a parody of Osamu Dazai. It makes reference to *No Longer Human,* but it still strikes me as a letter someone wrote hoping that someone would understand his true feelings."

"So then do you think it's true that he killed someone? And what about the part where he says he wishes he could die?"

"If it *is* true that he killed someone, that's bad."

In any case, "it seems like something is bothering Shuji" was now a contender for Understatement of the Century. He needed help urgently. Even if he was only under the delusion that he had killed somebody, anyone who would put that fantasy into writing was dangerous. I also doubted that a person could go on living for very long with such despair and self-loathing.

"Osamu Dazai committed suicide about a month after finishing *No Longer Human*. This might be serious."

The letter read like a suicide note. What had compelled Shuji Kataoka to give something like this to Takeda?

Perched on her fold-up chair hugging her knees, Tohko touched her right index finger to her lips and fell into deep thought.

"Dazai's story is composed of a foreword, three letters, and an afterword, and was serialized in three issues of a magazine. The foreword, which acts as a prologue to the story, and the first letter detailing the protagonist's childhood ran in the May issue. Less than a month after that, on June 13, he and his mistress, Tomie Yamazaki, drowned themselves in the Tama River."

Her lips moved mechanically, the rest of her face impassive.

"The second installment was published while the authorities were still dredging the river for their bodies. They finally found them on June 19. The third letter and the afterword, which served as the story's epilogue, were published one month later, in July. The story of *No Longer Human* seemed to be based on Dazai's life.

"The protagonist is born to an old aristocratic family in the countryside and feels fear and shame at his difference from other people, so he pretends to be a fool until finally throwing himself into dangerous social movements. But even that

is only an indifferent involvement, and he feels disgusted with himself. He carries on an indulgent lifestyle in order to escape his despair.

"In the midst of all that, he's implicated in a double suicide attempt with a waitress, which only he survives. He sinks into despair and denial. Even so, an angelic girl offers him her naïve trust and he takes her as his wife, managing some small happiness. But in the end he falls back into a life of poverty, introspection, and degradation.

"His wife's purity is sullied, the protagonist becomes addicted to drugs, and his friend commits him to a mental institution. He becomes more or less an invalid.

"The author, Osamu Dazai, was also born to a landowning family in the country and participated in social movements, but in the end, he tortured himself with the idea that he was nothing more than the coddled son of a fortunate family and attempted double suicide with a waitress.

"Dazai was saved, but the woman died. After that, he married Hatsuyo Oyama, a bar girl he sent for from his old country home. After discovering her transgressions against him, he was shocked and again attempted double suicide but failed. He became addicted to Pabinal and was admitted to a hospital.

"When he was released, he wrote *Human Lost*, the precursor to *No Longer Human*, and shortly thereafter attempted suicide with his wife, Hatsuyo, but that, too, ended in failure.

"Dazai went on to write many brilliant stories and was a fabulously active, popular author. He spent about ten years like that, then he completed *No Longer Human*. He committed double suicide immediately afterward, and this time neither Dazai nor his partner could be saved. That's why people think it was a suicide note."

Tohko trained her unfocused gaze on me and asked, "Have you read any of Dazai's stories, Konoha?"

"I've read *No Longer Human*. And I think parts of *Run, Melos!* and *Several Scenes of Mount Fuji* in a textbook."

"I've always wondered why they don't make an ethics textbook out of *Run, Melos!* It's a good story, sure, but there's just something *weird* about it. Ah-choo! Ah-choo! Ah-*choo!*"

She sneezed several times in succession, probably a by-product of talking for so long.

"Are you okay?"

"*Snf*, I'm fine... *hnk-nk*. So what did you think of Dazai?"

"I didn't really get it. It was nothing but monologue and a really gloomy story. I was really into *Run, Melos!* The ending was pretty convenient, and I think I was more surprised than moved by it. I only remember snapshots of *Scenes of Mount Fuji*, but I seem to remember thinking it was refreshing. That, and the style was rhythmical and easy to read. It almost felt like I was talking to the author."

"Exactly! That's one of the seductive things about Dazai's writing."

She blew her nose with a pink tissue, balled it up, and threw it in the trash before beginning another heated litany.

"There's a sense of affinity and immediacy in Dazai's works, as if the author is speaking directly to you. He dictated the story *An Urgent Appeal*, which is about Judas Iscariot, and it's the only one where there's pretty much nothing stopping the unfettered flow of his ideas, so it's really incredible. The potential second person in his narration gives rise to Dazai's greatest magic—that being the sympathy between author and reader."

"Sympathy?"

"Yes. Dazai was an author with divergent tastes. There are

people who won't read him because he's dark, or gloomy, or hesitant, but he has an unwavering charm for the people who like him. They fall for him completely. Even now, large numbers of people participate in a special memorial to mark Dazai's death once a year. I suspect that Dazai's fans could beat just about any other author's in their intensity.

"If you wonder why Dazai is so well-loved, it's because his readers see their own suffering in his stories.

"*I know how that feels. It's like that for me, too. This character is just like me.*... I'm sure you've had thoughts like that when you were reading before.

"There's a kind of magic in Dazai's stories that creates that sense of sympathy.

"Everybody in the world wants to be understood and to have others appreciate them.

"Being different is scary. Solitude is pain and loneliness. At times like that, Dazai's stories whisper seductively into your heart. As you move through the book, the reader and the writer become one and you fall headlong into the story beyond all escape. You start thinking, *Hey, he's talking about me. I'm the main character.*

"While he was still alive, Dazai received a lot of letters and journals from readers, pouring their hearts out to him. He even used parts of them to write some of his stories. The story *High School Girl* relates a day in the life of a perfectly ordinary girl, and it's taken almost word for word from the diary of Shizuko Ariake, on which it's based. She had been so influenced by Dazai's work that her writing style was identical to his. The diary could almost pass for one of his stories with only minor editing."

"Do you think Shuji related to *No Longer Human*, too, and that's why he wrote this letter?"

"Could be. He might have felt like the protagonist of the story. That's the power of Dazai's stories, but it can be frightening, too. If you read Dazai when you're depressed, you'll be dragged down into a sea of darkness..."

Perhaps Shuji Kataoka had also fallen under Dazai's spell and had been sucked under.

"But this letter isn't finished. I wonder if there are second and third installments, like in *No Longer Human*."

"Ah-choo! Geez, I hope not. If we don't find out whatever's bothering him before he writes the second letter, he might try to commit suicide with someone."

"Don't even joke about that..."

"I feel trapped just reading his letter, though. I wouldn't want to eat this even if I were starving. I bet it's like swallowing poison—it would make me want to die, too."

Tohko shuddered.

"I wonder who S is. Do you think the girl he talks about is... Takeda? And most of all, why can't we find Shuji Kataoka?"

"Yeah, that's the biggest problem. We have to find Shuji fast, and if he intends to commit double suicide or to kill someone, we have to stop him."

"But Takeda is still our only clue."

The next day was Saturday, so there was no school.

On Monday the following week, just like clockwork Takeda came skipping into my class during the first-period break.

"Did you write my letter for today yet, Konoha?"

She was even more grinny than usual. I cut her off with the seriousness of my tone. "Sorry, I couldn't write it. I won't be able to write any more unless I know more about Shuji."

The grin disappeared from Takeda's face. Now she looked more like an abandoned puppy

"Could you tell me about him? Everything you know. Then I'll write you a letter."

Takeda was silent, and she stared at her toes.

She fiddled with her interlaced fingers, then murmured, "Can you come to the library after school? I'll be in the storage room in the basement."

I descended a spiral staircase with clanging steps and met a gray door.

When I knocked, a voice called out, "Come in!"

As I cautiously pulled the door out, I caught a sweet scent.

It wasn't sweet like whipped cream or chocolate; it was the smell of old books.

The room was dusty and cobwebs stretched across the ceiling. There were a few rows of bookshelves and several stacked mounds of books on the floor.

It was like a graveyard for books. There was a space in the midst of it all just big enough for an old-style desk with a built-in chair. A lamp stood on the desk, providing the only illumination in the room.

Takeda was seated at the desk, apparently writing something. She shut her notebook with the duck picture and looked at me. She had a mug next to her, and it, too, was decorated with a drawing of a duck.

"There are cockroaches and mice in here," she said, a slight smile crossing her face.

I gawked at her and looked down at the floor.

"The librarians hate it here, too, so they hardly ever come down. But I like it. It's like my secret hideout."

"I...I see."

"Do you not like cockroaches, Konoha?"

"I don't think many people do."

"I guess you're right. There aren't a lot of cockroach fan clubs or Internet shrines."

"I think mice might be worse than cockroaches. When I was in elementary school, I stayed at my grandma's house in the country. When I woke up one morning, there was a dead mouse by my pillow and when I rolled over, I planted my face right on top of it. My grandma's cat had left it there. Urk, just thinking about it…"

Remembering the blood-spattered, still-warm body of the mouse, I shuddered.

"Oh, that's horrible. But it's fine, I *hardly ever* see any mice down here. If one comes out, I'll chase it away for you."

Takeda thumped her chest.

"Thanks. You're brave."

"Oh, would you like some tea, Konoha?"

Takeda took out an orange thermos, twisted the top off it, and poured out the amber liquid it contained.

"It's roasted green tea."

"Such refined taste."

She giggled. "Sometimes I come here to have some tea without anybody knowing."

It must have been the thermos's insulation that had kept the tea exactly the right temperature to drink.

"That was great. Thanks a lot." I set the lid on the desk and took Shuji's letter out of my pocket. "First, I want to return this to you."

Takeda accepted the letter from me without a word, slipped it into her duck notebook, then hugged them both to her chest.

"I hope you understand why I'm asking, but do you think maybe that letter was meant for someone else?"

Takeda's fingers dug into her notebook momentarily.

"There's no name on the envelope, and the tone of the letter doesn't seem like something intended for you."

"...You're right," Takeda said quietly. "Shuji didn't give me that letter. I found it by accident, stuck inside a book."

"In a book? Here?"

"Yes. It was inside a copy of *No Longer Human* by Osamu Dazai. I wondered what it was, so I read it, but I was so surprised. I couldn't stop thinking about it, and when I couldn't stand it anymore, I went to see Shuji."

"At archery?"

After a moment of hesitation, Takeda nodded firmly. "Yes."

"But there's no one named Shuji Kataoka on the team..."

"Yes, there is." Takeda raised her eyes, and her voice was firm. "I swear, Shuji really does exist."

I didn't get it. Why would Takeda continue to stand by Shuji Kataoka's existence?

Who was the person Takeda believed to be Shuji?

Or was it that Takeda was able to see him when none of us could? That would be some kind of horror movie.

Takeda set her notebook down on the desk and drooped dramatically.

A heavy silence filled the underground room.

I felt like I could almost hear the squeaking of the mice. I tried changing the subject.

"Did you know that the letter opens with a line from Dazai's *No Longer Human*?"

"...Yeah. After I read the letter, I borrowed *No Longer Human* and read it, too."

Takeda smiled weakly.

"But I'm too dumb... even after I read the book, I didn't understand why this person was suffering so much. He was from a

72

rich family and had servants, and every time his father went to Tokyo he brought back a present. His brothers and sisters adored him, his friends and teachers adored him, and he was smart and wrote things that everyone loved. Girls were all over him and he even had all those people commit double suicide with him, so why did he think he was an embarrassment as a human being? Why did he think his life had no value? That's... that's weird. It's deluded. There was no reason for him to ever suffer like that."

Takeda's eyes looked terribly desolate. She hung her head as she spoke, but she went on, her shoulders trembling and her lips reluctant to form the words.

"That's all I could think, which is awful, and I'm just an ordinary, dumb kid, really, really ordinary, just average and stupid, and so, so awful, so I couldn't understand why Osamu Dazai or Shuji would want to die, no matter how hard I tried. I read *No Longer Human* five times. But I still couldn't sympathize with them at all. Finally, I just started to cry."

Takeda's sadness crept into my heart.

She wanted to understand the boy she liked. But she couldn't.

I had also experienced that pain, of not understanding the heart of the person you cared for.

Takeda gulped, as if to swallow her tears, and pulled over her duck cup.

"A friend of mine named Shee gave me this cup for my birthday. She was my best friend, and really smart, unlike me. She could do anything. She told me this duck reminded her of me. Like how I'm clumsy and stupid and I get worked up over totally unimportant stuff, and how I'm so ordinary...

"I know I'll probably always be like this...I think that's probably why I was drawn to a person like Shuji, who seemed so dangerous.

"Honestly, I'm a dumb, regular kid. But if Shuji is in pain, I want to do something for him. I'll do anything I can."

She spoke with a heartfelt and powerful resolve.

Shuji did exist—inside Takeda, at least—and she earnestly cared for him.

So how could I argue with her?

"I didn't really understand *No Longer Human*, either," I murmured.

Takeda looked up at me with fragile eyes; she seemed to be on the verge of breaking down in tears. Her lips trembled slightly.

I thought she was going to throw herself on me like she had that day when it rained.

But Takeda gulped again and tugged the corners of her mouth into a smile.

"Heh! Ahaha...yeah! Commoners like us think he's a total jerk for being so ashamed of his privileges. Haha."

She was laughing as convincingly as she could, but it seemed like only empty cheer. Tears had filled her eyes by the end of it.

"Konoha...I really like your face."

"W-what? Come on."

She gazed at me with her tearful smile and murmured, "Your face is really pretty. It makes you look so kind."

People had teased me for looking like a girl before, but this was the first time anyone had actually called me pretty to my face. I was flustered.

"You're a weirdo, Takeda."

"Heh-heh! I have a request for you, Konoha. After school tomorrow, would you go to archery with me?"

I was surprised, so Takeda gave me one more push. "Please, come with me and meet Shuji."

S is dangerous.
S sees through everything.
S will probably destroy me.
Eventually, S will probably kill me.
What ecstasy that will be.

As I reread *No Longer Human* that night in my room, my mind wandered.

There's no Shuji Kataoka on the archery team, so who is Takeda taking me to meet? Or am I wrong?

It had been a few years since I'd read *No Longer Human*. It was still a story of suffering and hopelessness, but I must have grown up a little during the past few years and fallen out of step with everyone else because I felt as if I understood the protagonist's feelings better than when I'd last read it.

Oh, I remember that. It was like that for me, too. I realized those thoughts were drawing me into the story and my heart skipped a beat.

Oh man, Dazai's casting his spell on me, too.

"Konoha, you have a phone call."

My mom's voice sounded from downstairs.

I picked up the family phone. It was Tohko.

"Ah-choo! Hello, Konoha?"

Her cold had gotten worse, probably because she'd been pushing herself to come to school, and she'd gone home during second period. Before she left, she had staggered into my class and

scribbled her phone number on my hand, saying, "Here's my number. Take care of little Chia for me, okay? Don't get too emotional. Be nice to her, and if you see a ghost throw salt everywhere and then run. Call me right away if anything happens."

"*Ah-choo! Ah-choo!* Good, you made it home. Why didn't you call me? I was afraid that you'd been eaten by a ghost! *Ah-choo!*"

I stretched out on my bed and held my hand up to look at Tohko's phone number.

She didn't have to come all that way and then write it on me. I could have found it on the book club's member list (though it was only the two of us), but she'd grabbed my wrist and neatly written each number with a Sharpie. Her eyes had been unfocused the whole time, and I'd been shocked at how hot and sweaty her hand had been.

"I would have felt bad if you were snuggled up in bed asleep. How are you feeling?"

"I'm all better. But more important, what's going on with Chia?"

I knew I couldn't believe her when she said she was fine: I remembered times when she'd pushed herself too far before. But I told her about my conversation with Takeda.

She was surprised to hear that I was going with Takeda to visit the archery team tomorrow.

"Shuji's ghost might appear. Don't forget to take some salt with you, Konoha."

She was totally obsessed with ghosts. Did she know some ghosts personally? If there was such a thing as a goblin who eats books, I supposed it wouldn't be so strange if ghosts were real, too.

When I admitted that I'd been rereading *No Longer Human* and found myself getting into it, she sneezed and then chuckled.

"Whenever I'm com-*plete*-ly down in the dumps, that book can *bum. me. out.* Dazai's magic is serious stuff."

"When have you ever been depressed, Tohko?"

"How about when someone tells me I'm in a zone of romantic slaughter?"

"Haha."

"Or when everyone is eating fruit parfaits and I'm the only one who can't taste how good they are..."

I stopped laughing. The stuff that you and I eat is nothing more than tasteless sand to Tohko.

Not being able to taste the food that everyone around you swears is delicious must be so isolating. It's the exact same situation as the protagonist of *No Longer Human* who suffers because he can't feel what others feel.

Tohko sneezed again, then said in a cheerful voice, "I make do with my imagination. I just picture a superdelicious book, and then I can talk about how delicious everything is, too."

"You're such a book girl."

"Heh-heh. You got it. Oh, but there's one part of *No Longer Human* that I can never relate to."

"What's that?"

"When he says, 'I don't have any concept of what it means to feel hunger.' No matter how hard I try to imagine it, I can't understand that at all....Man, talking to you made me hungry. Ah-*choo!*"

Even when she was sick or depressed, apparently Tohko never changed much.

I told her she needed to take vitamin C for her cold, then hung up.

A book rich in vitamin C—I wondered what kind of book that would be.

*   *   *

Tohko stayed home from school the next day. I guess she was trying to take care of herself.

After classes ended, Takeda came looking for me.

"All right, Konoha, let's go!"

She was so excited, I might have thought we were going to an amusement park.

"What's this, Inoue? A date?"

"No way!"

My classmates teased us, but I gently deflected it with a smile.

Kotobuki was glaring at me frigidly. Maybe she thought I was a two-faced liar because I'd told her that Takeda and I weren't dating.

Takeda was dragging me from the room, and we headed out.

"You're sure Shuji is on the archery team?"

"Why are you asking me such a silly question after all this time? Of course he is!"

And what exactly was so silly about that question?

I was still wary when we arrived at the archery team's practice hall.

"Hello, everybody! Do you mind if we watch?" Takeda called out brightly at the entrance to the hall.

"Hey, it's Chia! Where've you been?"

"Hey, is that your boyfriend? Chia, I'm shocked!"

The team members came over and started talking to her as if they knew her well. I couldn't argue with the fact that Takeda apparently came here all the time.

Which I guess means that she came here to see Shuji...

This was just getting more confusing.

Team members brought over two chairs for us.

Each time an arrow hit the bull's-eye, Takeda would applaud and shout, "Wow! Amazing! Nice shot!"

78

A little ways into practice, Akutagawa appeared in his uniform. When he saw me, he made a weird face.

I nodded slightly to him, and he returned the gesture. I'm sure he was only acting true to his character by not gossiping with someone from his class, but I was embarrassed that he thought I'd come to watch the practice with a date.

I whispered to Takeda, "So which one is Shuji?"

"I'm lookiiing. Ohhh, it's him!"

Takeda pointed.

I was blown away. The person she was pointing at was Akutagawa, currently drawing his bow. His back was perfectly straight and his face intent; he looked awesome.

"*What?* Akutagawa is Shuji?"

"Whaaaaaat? You *know* him, Konoha?"

"He's in my class. How can Akutagawa be Shuji? He's a second-year student, and he's so serious. I can't believe he's ever told a joke in his entire life."

"Yeah, that's true. He's what you would call 'stoic,' right?"

"Huh? So Akutagawa isn't Shuji?"

Takeda bubbled with laughter. "Of course he isn't! I just wanted to show you who was the best shooter on the team!"

Twang!

Akutagawa's arrow embedded itself in the center of the target.

"Eeee! Bull's-eye! That was great!" Takeda leapt to her feet to cheer for him. "See? He's really good, isn't he?"

I fumed. "Takeda, we are *not* spies from another school here to do reconnaissance on the archery team's practice, and we are *not* here to do a story for the school paper on who the hottest members of the archery team are."

"I know *that!* We're here so we can see Shuji."

"So where is he?"

"Let's see..."

Takeda scanned the practice hall from end to end.

Just then, four or five adults came in.

"Hey, there, kids! You practicing hard?"

"Oh, it's Manabe!"

"The alums are here, everybody!"

"Hello, Mister Manabe."

"Hey, Kashiwagi. You improved any since last time?"

"Yes! I practiced like you said, and now my arrows go exactly where I want them to."

"Great, I'll have to see that."

"Thanks!"

"Soeda and Rihoko, too! You haven't been back to visit for a while."

"Well, we're here to bother you again."

"Heh-heh, it really has been a long time. So many memories!"

"I heard you're going to have a baby, Rihoko. Congratulations!"

"Thanks. I've still got a while to go, though. I stopped working last week, so now I have lots of time on my hands. I'll be right back here next month!"

"You sure, Rihoko? You shouldn't push yourself."

"You're such a worrier, Manabe."

Apparently the alumni had come to watch the team practice. There was one woman among the men.

"Once a month, some alumni come back and mentor the team," Takeda explained. "That handsome man with the mustache is Mister Manabe. He was captain ten years ago when they placed second in a national competition. The members from back then still get together and keep an eye on their successors, I guess."

"How'd you find all that out?"

"Because I've been coming here all the time to watch, of course. I'm like the team's cheerleader now," Takeda said proudly.

We'd gotten off topic again. When was I gonna see Shuji?

Just then, I heard a voice that was tense with fear.

"Shuji—!"

I quickly scanned the area.

Shuji had finally appeared!

But no matter which way I looked, I didn't see any likely candidates.

"Shuji? That's impossible!"

"There's no way."

Other people were crying out in fearful voices.

Where was he? *Where?*

Suddenly I smelled sweat and tobacco; I felt hands on either side of my face and I was pulled out of my chair.

The man with the mustache was staring down at me, his eyes so wide it seemed they would pop from their sockets. It was Manabe, the alum.

"Shuji…"

The name slipped huskily from Manabe's nicotine-stained lips as his eyes devoured me.

I was stupefied.

I…was Shuji?

Was he saying that Shuji Kataoka was *me?*

Manabe's hands dropped away from my cheeks, which had grown cold as ice.

"No…you're not him," he murmured weakly, the fire vanished from his eyes. "You couldn't be, of course…Shuji is—I'm sorry. You just looked like someone I knew. Are you with the school paper?"

"No, I'm here to watch the practice. I'm a second-year student."

The group of alumni had surrounded me, all of them looking at me as if they'd seen a ghost.

It disturbed me to be the object of such looks, and I shuddered.

Why were they looking at me like that? And why had they said that I looked like Shuji Kataoka?

"He really does resemble Kataoka," the woman whispered fiercely. "Kataoka was a little taller, but…your face is exactly the same. You could be Kataoka's brother. What's your name?"

"K-Konoha Inoue."

"Konoha? That's an unusual name. But it's sweet. Is there anyone in your family named Kataoka?"

"Hey, leave him alone, Rihoko."

One of the alums, an intellectual-looking man wearing glasses and a suit, interrupted the woman—Rihoko.

"But Konoha might have some connection to Shuji. They look so alike."

"Not that alike. It's been so long since we've seen Shuji that the memory has faded, so we think that some boy who vaguely resembles him is his twin."

"Yeah…you may be right, Soeda."

"Manabe…"

Rihoko's face stilled.

"Um—" I ventured impetuously. "What sort of person was Shuji Kataoka?"

The group of alumni turned and regarded me as one. Then they looked at each other uncomfortably.

"Kataoka was actually quite a troublemaker," Rihoko said suddenly. "He took the easy way out and didn't take anything seriously, and the only reason he ever spoke up was to tell a joke."

"Cut it out, Rihoko," Manabe stopped her. Then he looked at me with a pained smile. "Shuji was on the archery team with us."

With them!

So Shuji was a graduate of the archery team, too, just like Manabe and the rest.

Shuji Kataoka did exist.

But not on the current archery team—he had been on the team years ago.

I glanced over to see how Takeda was taking this. She was staring at the alumni, round-eyed.

Huh? Hadn't she known that Shuji was a graduate? Or had she gotten a crush on him without realizing that? I suppose that might be possible.

"What's he doing now?"

What sort of man had Shuji Kataoka become, from the boy who had constantly felt "dread at the fact that my own concept of happiness fails to mesh with the rest of the world's view of the same emotion," who had therefore decided to don the mask of a mime?

Beside me, I heard Takeda's breath catch.

Manabe's face grew even gloomier.

"We aren't going to see Shuji again. I'm sorry, it's not a very pleasant story. Let's leave it at that. I'm truly sorry to have startled you, Konoha."

"Let's get back to practice!" the man in the glasses said brightly, and no one said anything more about Shuji.

The alums split off to mentor the kids, leaving Takeda and me by ourselves.

Takeda fixated on the targets with a strained expression on her face.

Her face was hard and strong—and *intent*—as if she were look-ing at a hated enemy.

"Takeda?"

She looked at me, and her face was horribly empty.

"…I'm sorry. It looks like Shuji isn't coming today."

Chapter 4 – One Bright Day in May, He...

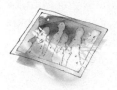

Why don't I tell you about S?

S was the person who understood me better than any in the world, was my nemesis, my best friend, my other half, my eternal opponent.

The terrifying wisdom S possessed penetrated everything.

My act, which hoodwinked everyone I ever met, failed to convince S.

I feared S accordingly.

The more fear I felt of S, the less I was able to escape.

In classes and after, I was with S.

I felt as though S's gaze was a judge employed by God to check me—a thought which caused my limbs to tremble and sweat to break out with fear and shame.

This world is hell.

I was a slave to S.

⟫◆⟪

I spent lunch the next day scouring through old yearbooks at the library.

I sat down at a table in the reading room and flipped through the album from ten years ago.

There was a picture of the archery team taken after they'd placed in the national tournament. There was the young Manabe without his mustache, the man with the glasses, and even Rihoko, all of them smiling and holding certificates and a trophy.

There was no one who looked like Shuji Kataoka.

I turned next to the class photos.

It gave me a strange feeling to examine each person's face in turn, searching for someone who looked like me.

Class one, class two, class three, class four...

When I turned the next page, I felt as if a cold hand had just stroked the back of my neck.

There he was.

In the group photo for class five of the third-year students.

The students' names were listed below it, and the name Shuji Kataoka was among them.

But in this, the critical photo, I could not find his face. There was space at the top of the page where it looked like a photo had been pasted in.

That part had been neatly cut out.

What did it mean that his picture had been up there?

And who in the world would have cut it out and taken it?

A shiver ran though me.

Maybe Shuji transferred to another school before graduation. Or maybe...maybe he was in the hospital because he got sick or hurt, so he couldn't be in the class picture. Or maybe...

I closed the yearbook and moved to the computer room: I wanted to try an Internet search on Shuji Kataoka and the school's name from ten years ago.

I found an old newspaper article.

Reading it made me feel dizzy.

Ten years ago in May, Shuji Kataoka (seventeen), a third-year student at Seijoh Academy, had jumped off a roof to his death.

The words "jumped off a roof" dug icy claws into my heart, beating violently against the gates of old memories.

It was too much.

My throat was dry, my head spinning.

Of all things, a roof.

And he jumped off, of all things.

It was terrible.

The article said that he had stabbed himself in the chest with a knife just before jumping. It mentioned that his death was believed to be a suicide because of a note left at his home.

I felt sick to my stomach, thinking about the insurmountable regrets and despair in his life.

Why did it always have to be like this?

Before we had discovered the second letter, Shuji Kataoka had taken his own life, just like Osamu Dazai.

"No way! How could Shuji have killed himself ten years ago?"

At book club after school, Tohko was just as floored as I had been when she heard my news.

"I wonder if Chia knows about this."

"I don't know," I murmured dispassionately.

I had felt dizzy and nauseous when I read the article about Shuji's suicide at the library, and I'd been terrified that maybe *that* was going to kick in again, but the chaos had receded like a wave, leaving only questions.

"It shouldn't be possible to meet someone who's been dead for ten years, so that means that Takeda has been lying to us. Why

would she have done that? What benefit does she get from doing something like that?"

"It may have something to do with the fact that you resemble Shuji. Are you sure there's no one in your family named Kataoka?"

"I'm sure. At least, no one I've ever heard of."

The day that Takeda had run past, crying in the rain, she had called me "Shuji." She had known that I resembled him.

So then why had she spent so much time with me?

Tohko held one end of her braids in each hand, then sprang to her feet.

"Oh, maybe! You and Shuji might be brothers! Shuji's suicide could just be an act, and in fact he'd secretly gotten mixed up in a terrible plot. Relatives after his inheritance turned their sights on you, the rightful heir to the company, and they sent a string of assassins after you. Little Chia is actually your bodyguard, and, and, and..."

"Cut it out. That's such cheap story development."

Tohko slumped. "I'm sorry. It just came to me."

"I think your brain got cooked when you were sick."

"That's so mean! I'm all better now. And besides, my hunches might not be all wrong, you know!"

"Hunches? That wasn't a hunch, it was total delusion."

"Hmmph."

Tohko scowled and puffed out her cheeks grumpily.

"Oh, I know. We need to investigate this case in depth. My hunches might be *just a tiny bit* right."

"How are we going to investigate something from ten years ago?"

"We could ask teachers who were here ten years ago, or ask old book club members. There are ways to do it."

"*Are* there old book club members?"

Tohko puffed up her flat chest and pulled out a notebook.

"Ha! This volume contains the names of former members of Seijoh Academy's legendary book club. Let's see, alumni from ten years ago...Look! There's three whole people!"

That's it?

"Let's get in touch with them ASAP."

Tohko hurried me out of the club room, surging with excitement. There was a pay phone on the first floor. Tohko kept one eye on the notebook as she dialed each number. Tohko didn't own a cell phone, since her body (I guess?) messed up machines. I didn't carry mine with me much, since I didn't have that many friends.

We called the first name on the list.

"This telephone number is no longer in service. Please confirm the number you have dialed and..."

Then the second one: "Huh? Kobayashi? My name is Kakimoto."

Then the third one: "Ahaha, well now, *our* baby boy went to work at a laboratory in Paris last spring. Ahaha!"

"W-well, there's still the first- and second-year students from ten years ago."

Tohko flipped through the notebook, smiling.

The first of the second-year students: *"This call cannot be completed due to customer problems."*

The second: "Huh? Book club? Everything's going to hell right now. Call me back in six months. *CLICK!*"

Next were the first-year students...

"There aren't any. No first-year students. It's blank."

Tohko looked at the empty column on the list of names and stuck out her lower lip.

The greater mystery was not the truth of who Shuji Kataoka was, but how our club had ever managed to survive.

Standing in front of the phone, shoulders slumped, Tohko nervously fiddled with the tip of one braid. I spoke up soberly. "Let's forget about it. We're better off not getting involved with Takeda or Shuji more than we already are."

The truth was, after I found out that Shuji had leaped to his death, I'd gotten scared. The roof brought back bad memories.

Tohko looked back over her shoulder at me, her eyes ever so slightly sad. "Can you live with that, Konoha?"

"Well, it creeps me out that my doppelgänger committed suicide, and it bothers me that Takeda and the archery team alums are all hiding something. But what can I do about it?"

Tohko frowned dejectedly. Then she shook her head fiercely, her braids swinging together like cats' tails. "No, I can't do it. What if Shuji's ghost wants us to find out the truth, and he's reaching out to us from the beyond? If we quit now, he'll never be at peace and I'll never get that lovely report from little Chia!"

If Shuji was in the beyond, didn't that mean he was already at peace? This was about food, after all...

I was deflated, but Tohko grabbed my arm and resolutely declared, "We can't let this defeat us! Let's dig a little deeper. For this... for *this*... I'm willing to take it all off."

Wha—?

The next day we visited the school's music hall.

It belonged to the school orchestra, so it was never used for classes. According to the stories, the former members of the orchestra and their fan club had pooled their money to have it built.

The orchestra had a lot of members and every year they earned high scores at national competitions. Former members were active around the world, and the school director and his son had both belonged to it.

Because of that, the orchestra was in a class all its own, even among the more well-populated clubs. The difference between it and the two-member book club that was allowed to use a spare storage room out of pity was like the difference between a mansion with an elaborate security system and a run-down apartment with no bathroom.

We opened the thick, soundproofed door and went inside. The first thing we saw was a huge hall that could have seated a thousand people. Musicians with violins, violas, and cellos were practicing under the tutelage of a professional coach.

The variety of sounds pounded against my ears like an invisible flood.

"Wow...so this is the entire orchestra."

I'd thought the archery team had a lot of members, but the orchestra was an even bigger clan. In one quick glance, I thought I counted a hundred people.

"Hmph. More members don't make a better club," Tohko observed sourly beside me.

There were several small rooms other than the big hall, and a member of the orchestra guided us to one of these.

"This is it."

"Thanks. We can handle the rest."

"All right. Excuse me, then."

When our guide had left, Tohko squared her shoulders as if to harden her resolve, then opened the door. "Here I am, Maki!"

Instantly, the smell of art supplies assaulted me.

What's going on?

Bright sunlight came in through a skylight to illuminate the room. One entire wall was covered with painted canvases and sketches on paper. A canvas was propped up on an easel in the center of the room, where a girl in a school uniform sat holding a paintbrush. She turned to look at us and grinned slyly.

"Great! So you didn't back out."

In the light, her brown hair gleamed golden, and I squinted reflexively in the face of such brilliance.

Her features were also sharply impressive, and she was taller than many boys. She made a majestic picture. And unlike Tohko, she had a chest and curves; there was a sensuality to her body and her entire frame gave off a powerful aura.

This was Maki Himekura.

The school director's granddaughter and the conductor in charge of the orchestra. The princess who was always the subject of gossip, with her illustrious heritage and good looks.

"So that's Konoha, huh? Isn't he a cutie. I'm Maki Himekura. You can call me Maki."

When she turned her powerful, luminous eyes on me, I tensed.

"It's very nice to meet you, Maki."

She gave me a look after that awkward response and grinned.

Everyone called her "the princess" and gave her special treatment at school, but she didn't possess so much as a shred of meekness or hesitation.

I knew that was because, unlike me, she was the real thing. After she'd had her fill of me, Maki turned to Tohko and her eyes narrowed with pleasure.

"Heh-heh. It was pretty gutsy of you to bring Konoha along, Tohko. You do know what we're going to be doing, don't you?"

Tohko pouted prettily. "Did you find out what I asked you to?"

"It's all here. Because unlike you, we have alums to burn. We've got contact info for more people than we have time to call."

"W-we only let a tiny elite into the book club!"

"Uh-huh. In any case, the orchestra makes up the majority of the Academy's alumni. There are even members with influence in the police department, so I was able to discover quite a lot about Shuji Kataoka."

"Ohhh, like what?"

The corner of Maki's mouth lifted in a smirk, and she leered at Tohko suggestively.

"That information will be exchanged for the condition we discussed. Are you prepared, Tohko?"

"Geez, all right already…"

"Then take your clothes off and sit in that chair. Oh, you can change the pose however you want. I'll just go ahead and sketch it."

"Urk."

Tohko's cheeks flushed red and she touched the ribbon at her throat with slender fingers.

"Hold on, what are you guys talking about? What are you planning to do?"

I couldn't process what the condition was, and the girls each looked at me with different emotions: Tohko with embarrassment, Maki with relish.

"I'm going to model for one of her pictures."

"Right. Nude."

N-n-*NUDE?!*

"I've had my eye on her since we started here, and I've kept trying to convince her to do it. I just *had* to draw a picture of Tohko before we graduated. Only a natural state will do for a true beauty; dressing her up and decorating her with accessories would only distract. I totally scored when you finally changed your mind!"

Tohko's face was bright red, and she was cringing. "Hey, you never said I had to get totally naked! Th…that depends on your information."

"Which means if I've got good info, you agree to go all the way?"

"I…haven't decided."

"Heh-heh-heh, Well, in any case, let's get started. Oh, why don't you take a seat over there, Konoha? Then you can fully appreciate the view."

"I said I wasn't doing nude!"

I calmly replied, "Tohko has no breasts to speak of. She's perfectly flat-chested. Are you sure you want to use her?"

"Konoha!"

"Oh my. Have you already seen Tohko naked?"

"You can tell that much with her clothes on. There's not a bump on her. I think someone with more curves would make a better model."

"You're sooo mean! I...might not have much, but there's at least *something* there! I'm not totally flat!"

Maki sputtered, then hugged her stomach and exploded into laughter.

"Ahahaha! Hah...hahahaha! You're an interesting one, little man. You're right, Tohko is com-*plete*-ly flat...Hahahaha!"

"Maki, if you don't stop laughing this instant, I'm leaving!"

"Mmf...heh-heh...understood."

"Geez, everyone makes fun of me."

Pouting angrily, Tohko tugged her ribbon from her shirt.

Then she popped her top button open, and her pale white collarbone flashed into sight.

"But you know, Tohko, I really am ecstatic to be able to draw this picture of you."

Maki crossed her legs and propped her open sketchbook on one knee, then turned a sharp eye on Tohko.

"I wanted to join the art club, not orchestra. But Grandpa and the others forced me into it because of their stupid tradition. I got this room as my condition for joining the orchestra. Half the time I'm here drawing pictures after school. I find an interesting

subject and study its every aspect. The time I spend here in trial and error trying to render something's true form is nearly heaven for me."

Her voice was impassioned as she sketched Tohko's figure with a charcoal pencil.

Tohko was sitting on a chair with one knee drawn up. She pulled the shoe off her foot and *plunked* it onto the floor.

Then she took her sock off, too. With a smooth whisper, her pale ankle and beautifully aligned toes were revealed. The nails were painted the same light pink as her fingernails.

Resting her cheek on her knee, Tohko murmured in a calm tone so utterly unlike her usual voice, "Tell me, Maki. Did Shuji really commit suicide? Before he fell off the roof, he stabbed a heavy-duty knife into his chest, right? Isn't it possible someone else stabbed him?"

Her hand never stopping, Maki replied, "Apparently they pursued the theory that it was a homicide, too, but they only found Shuji's fingerprints on the knife. Besides, he had a motive for suicide, and they found a note at his house. That's what made the police decide it was a suicide."

"He had a motive?"

With another whisper, Tohko unraveled one of her braids and fanned her hair out. Her glossy black hair rippled like a soft wave in the ocean. I leaned forward, feeling as if it were sucking me in.

Maki took in a soft breath.

Tohko's expression was shockingly mature. Her lips were loosely closed and she looked straight at Maki with an almost drowsy expression.

Who knew Tohko was capable of looking so...sexy?

"At...the time, Shuji was dating a girl named Sakiko Kijima. Apparently they were a good couple. Sakiko was a beautiful girl,

kind and soft-spoken, and they say that Shuji loved her very much and would gush about her to anyone. Shuji liked to give people more than they asked for anyway, and he talked in a cheerful, offhanded way to everyone, so whenever anyone asked him about Sakiko, he would go on forever about where they'd gone on a date or what they'd talked about on the phone the night before. He'd talk about anything.

"Sakiko was completely devoted to Shuji, too. Apparently she would wait for him after archery, and the two of them would go home hand in hand every day."

Plunk.

Tohko dropped her other shoe onto the floor.

"But one day right after they'd started their third year, Shuji stayed late for team business. Sakiko went home by herself for once and, as luck would have it, she was hit by a car and killed."

"That's awful…Really?" Tohko murmured, her eyes still drowsing.

"The light was red and everything, but Sakiko apparently ran out into the road anyway. She was hit by a truck coming around a curve. They said she was killed instantly."

Tohko said nothing and only unraveled her other braid. Waves of black hair spilled down to her waist, cloaking her slender body bewitchingly. She embodied a muse of the arts.

I felt my throat parch suddenly.

"I wonder why Sakiko tried to cross the road when the light was red."

"Who knows? Maybe she was hurrying on her way to an errand. Or maybe she didn't see any cars, so she thought it was safe. In any case, Sakiko died and Shuji lost the love of his life. They say he suffered more than a little because he blamed himself for not

going home with her like they always had. One month later...he killed himself."

The image of a boy falling off the roof started running through my mind. The tips of my fingers tingled and my mouth drew tight.

Uh-oh.

It had happened ten years ago. It was utterly unrelated to *that.*

I struggled to get my breathing under control so Tohko and Maki wouldn't realize that anything unusual was happening.

Tohko asked her next question philosophically. "What was in the suicide note they found at Shuji's house?"

"That it was his fault she was dead, that he couldn't bear to live without her, that he was going to be with her soon. And then—" Maki stopped abruptly.

Pop.

Tohko undid a second button.

"He apologized for ever being born."

I felt as if I could hear his voice in my mind, and goose bumps prickled my skin.

Tohko rested her face on her knees and touched her index finger to her lips thoughtfully.

Fighting back the tightness in my chest, I asked, "What exactly was Shuji Kataoka like?"

"He was easygoing and always telling jokes or messing around. Really popular. Whenever he was around, people couldn't stop laughing. But then, when he was alone he looked very serious and a little brooding. Girls love that kind of thing. And they really went for him, apparently. They say he was a very kind person...and that the look of shame he sometimes got was unbelievably hot.

"They said so many girls would flock around him during

archery that they couldn't actually practice and the manager scolded him all the time. But he would just laugh it off, which made the manager even angrier, and then *everyone* would laugh. As you can imagine, it was always a lot of fun with Shuji around."

It was exactly the same image of Shuji that Takeda had first given us.

A cheerful, fun, and kind upperclassman.

Usually upbeat, but whenever he was shooting an arrow, his face became hard.

But the effervescent, popular boy was a mime's disguise that he himself had created and not the real him. In the letter Takeda had shown me, he had said over and over that he was a monster incapable of loving people. He was ashamed to be alive, he couldn't stand for everyone to find out, he swore he would rather die first.

The letter had been stuck inside a copy of Osamu Dazai's *No Longer Human*.

Why had Shuji prepared a second, different suicide note?

Who was the letter intended for?

Maybe for S, the person who understood him and who was going to destroy him?

Or was it for someone else?

Tohko undid the third button on her shirt.

Pale, white skin and a glimpse of white lace peeked out from the opening in her jacket shirt, making my heart pound.

"Did Shuji have any particularly close friends?"

Maki's hand never stopped moving as she stared hungrily at Tohko.

"Apparently he had quite a lot of close friends; but *particularly* close... that's harder. There were Shigeru Manabe and Yasuyuki

Soeda, who were in his class and on the archery team with him. Apparently the three of them were together a lot. Manabe was their leader, Soeda was the sage and lackey, and Shuji was the one who caused all the trouble and other fun. At the time, Manabe was dating the team's manager, Rihoko Sena, and they and Sakiko would all go out. After graduation, Rihoko broke up with Manabe and started dating Soeda. They got married, so now she's Rihoko Soeda."

Shigeru Manabe. Yasuyuki Soeda. Rihoko Sena. And his girlfriend, Sakiko Kijima.

All of their names started with "S."

"Oh, and I got a picture of him for you guys."

Maki paused in her drawing and held the photo up, its face turned toward her. Then she asked meaningfully, "Wanna see it?"

"You deviant," Tohko muttered, defeated. She unfastened her fourth button.

A smile came over Maki's face, but she didn't move.

The front of the shirt was completely open, exposing the slip that covered Tohko's chest. A pale violet bra showed through the white silk. I didn't know what to do with my eyes.

When Maki still didn't move, color flashed into Tohko's cheekbones.

"I'm just getting over a cold, you know. If I take off any more, I'll get sick again."

"If that happens, I'll make arrangements for you to stay in a private room at the hospital my family goes to and nurse you back to health myself.

"C'moo-n. If you don't show me, the deal's off." Tohko pouted.

I spoke up.

"Tohko looks like such a kid, it's basically breaking the deal

anyway. Even if she takes off more, it's not going to magically give her a chest. She's amazingly flat, even with the slip."

Just then, I felt a nearby canvas hit me in the head.

"Oh my God! I hate you, Konoha!"

The mature aura that had surrounded Tohko had evaporated. She held a canvas in both hands and swung it at me again, shouting at me with tears in her eyes. "Hate you, hate you, hate yoooou!"

"Hey, Tohko, try to be careful with that. Guess I've got no choice."

Maki flipped the picture around.

Tohko stopped hitting me and we both leaned forward to examine it.

The picture showed three boys and two girls dressed in the school's old uniforms, before they'd changed styles. The boy with the brashly confident expression was Manabe, the intellectual-looking boy in the glasses was Soeda, and the strong-willed beauty was Rihoko. The pale, slender girl in the center was probably Sakiko Kijima. And the boy shyly holding Sakiko's hand was Shuji Kataoka.

Long bangs fell across his face and he wore an easy smile on his girlish face.

He was taller and looked more grown-up than me.

But other than that...

I gulped in surprise. Tohko's eyes went wide, too.

"He looks exactly like you, Konoha..."

It was true: Shuji Kataoka looked so much like me he could have been my uncle, or even my older brother.

⇒◆⇐

When I think back to how S and I became closer, I see it was an odd thing.

At first, S hated me and would glare at me and speak sharply.

Even when I donned my clown costume and everyone laughed, S alone watched me in irritation.

S saw through everything.

That thought chilled me to the core and caused me such dismay that I could have groveled, dragging my belly over the ground like a dog.

And so I insinuated myself with S, acting even more foolish, even more incompetent, even more submissive, in my attempt to mold S's opinion of me.

S did begin to laugh at me, almost in resignation. Perhaps it was out of pity. I crept ever closer to S, worshipped and swore my false allegiance to S. To our friends, we thus became the master and the slave.

But the fact that S was my enemy never changed.

Sometimes S would condemn my clowning with a pitying look or an indifferent attitude. When S told me outright that I was lying, I felt as if a chasm yawned open at my feet and I was about to tumble in headlong.

Had I committed a sin? By being born in this wretched body that contained no human emotion? Incapable of grief or adoration, I had merely staged a dangerous performance. Was all of that my fault? Yes, I suppose it must have been.

Sin has been a part of me since birth; I am Cain wearing his brother's skin. Why shouldn't I be reproached for that? Whatever I do, I can only suffer.

What does S want from me?

To stop acting the clown?

To reveal my monstrosity to the world and suffer the stones they would hurl at me?

But S knows nothing! Not the pain that burns through the

body of a person born as a monster, nor the fear. S knows none of it—none of it!

Just now I felt such powerful hatred for S's "righteousness" that I choked with its heat.

———⋙◆⋘———

How much did Takeda know about Shuji Kataoka?

The next day, I sat at my desk during the third-period break and thought about everything that had happened.

Takeda hadn't come to see me again today.

What in the world had she been thinking? What had she hoped to achieve?

And why had Shuji Kataoka committed suicide after his girlfriend's death?

When I'd read his second suicide note, I was struck by how much he had suffered because of the shallowness of his affection for other people.

If it wasn't the death of his girlfriend, then what had convinced him to kill himself?

I didn't really understand the part of his letter where he talked about killing someone.

It was possible that he had written that because he felt some responsibility for Sakiko's death, but it read as if he had witnessed someone else's death firsthand.

It was hopeless. There were too many mysteries. Maybe there was a second installment somewhere, like in *No Longer Human*. Maybe it would be stuck inside another of Dazai's books. But no, if that were the case, someone would have already found it. Wait a second . . .

A question suddenly occurred to me.

Takeda said that she found Shuji's letter inside a copy of *No Longer Human*.

But Shuji had jumped to his death ten years ago.

Wasn't it strange that the letter had escaped notice for ten whole years? People must have been borrowing *No Longer Human* all the time, too.

I felt someone's eyes on me and looked up.

Kotobuki was standing right in front of me, glaring. It looked like she had something to say to me.

"My change?" she snapped.

"Huh?"

"You haven't paid back my ten yen yet."

"Oh! Uh, sorry."

I'd forgotten all about it. I dug my wallet out frantically, but unfortunately, I didn't have a ten-yen coin. "Umm..."

"It's fine. Later."

"Sorry..."

Well, that was totally awkward. But seriously, why wouldn't she just get over ten yen?

Kotobuki didn't move, so I guess there was more she wanted to unload on me. Her cheeks were flushed, and she kept shifting her eyes around, looking torn. Finally she burst out, "Hey, did you know that Takeda is going out with a first-year boy? I hear they're all over each other."

"Wha—?"

I gaped, and Kotobuki went on coolly. "It's true. I asked a first-year at student council. They've been together since April, and they eat lunch together in the yard every day. I guess she was two-timing you, Inoue. Oh, but you and Takeda weren't dating, were you? So I guess you wouldn't care."

"Thanks for letting me know."

Kotobuki was surprised. I'm sure I must have had a scary look on my face.

The bell rang and Kotobuki reminded me once more about returning her ten yen before she all but ran away. She looked as though she was on the verge of tears, but I didn't have time to worry about that.

So Takeda was dating a first-year boy? What was going on?

I went out to the school yard at lunchtime.

White clouds floated in the May sky overhead and the breeze was warm. Students were scattered here and there with their lunches. In their midst, I spotted Takeda and her first-year boyfriend.

They sat next to each other on the grass and had their lunch boxes spread out in their laps on napkins.

The napkins were part of a set in different colors: Takeda's was pink, and the boy's was blue. Their lunch boxes looked like they matched, too, but the boyfriend's was one size bigger.

Takeda was talking animatedly to her boyfriend.

"Aren't these shrimp dumplings great, Hiro? I made them fresh, y'know."

"They're the best I ever had! They're still crisp and every-thing."

"Heh-heh. I seasoned them with pepper. And there's a little bit of onion in it. Goes well with the rice, right?"

"Yeah. You're such a good cook, Chee."

"I tried extra hard for you, Hiro."

"Hey, Chee, I don't have basketball practice on Sunday. You wanna see a movie?"

"Oh wow! Absolutely! Hurray, this is our fourth date!"

The boy blushed; he seemed to be the one who'd come chasing

after Takeda the day it had rained. He had the look of a jock, with his short hair and simple face.

The two of them chatted sweetly. They were every inch the infatuated couple.

"Oh—"

Takeda's face froze as soon as she noticed me.

I hadn't done anything wrong, but my ears and cheeks burned. I felt bad, and embarrassed. I stared at Takeda, then turned and hurried back to my classroom.

What's up with that?

Seriously, what was that?

When classes were over, I stepped out of my classroom to head for the book club. Takeda was waiting for me in the hall.

She was just squirming and didn't say a word, so I walked right past her in silence.

"Err—"

Takeda trailed after me.

I kept walking in silence for a while; then, without turning around, I coldly asked, "What?"

She didn't answer.

"Did you come to explain about your boyfriend?"

"H-Hiro is..."

"I heard you've been dating since April. Every day you eat homemade lunches in the yard and you've been on three dates already. Do I have that right?"

Even I thought I was being mean, but I couldn't contain my indignation.

For the last two weeks I'd been writing love letters and going to the archery club and pulling out old yearbooks at the library, doing everything I could to help Takeda out.

When I'd seen Takeda talk about Shuji with such exuberance,

I thought it would be nice if she could convey those feelings to him. Takeda had come every day to give an eager report on how things were going with him. It was embarrassing when she did it in front of my classmates, but I'd been thrilled for her. When Takeda swore through tears that she wanted to do whatever she could to help Shuji, my heart ached with hers.

But now I find out she's had a boyfriend since April? That they were all over each other?

Give me a break.

I came to a stop on the landing of the stairwell and glared at Takeda.

Takeda shrunk down and stared at her feet.

"Why did you pretend to have a crush on an upperclassman on the archery team? What exactly were you trying to get me to do?"

Takeda was silent, apparently pained.

"It's all right if you don't want to answer. Everything else you've ever said to me has been a lie. Shuji Kataoka is dead. He jumped off a roof ten years ago."

When I said that, Takeda looked up in surprise. I knew there was nothing to be gained by continuing to be so harsh to her, but the words kept coming.

"Shuji Kataoka only exists in your delusions. I'm done being jerked around by you. It's beyond creepy that a guy who looks exactly like me jumped off a building ten years ago. I just want to forget all about it. Don't ever come to my class again."

I turned my back on Takeda and went up the stairs. Takeda called out in a strangled voice, "S-someone like you...could never understand!"

When I turned back around, Takeda was staring up at me desolately.

Something about her face reminded me of the last look another girl I'd known had given me. It caught me off-guard.

Miu!

Takeda bit her lip and looked down, then ran down the stairs. It was a long time before I could move from that spot.

"Konoha, I don't think you would ever understand."

Chapter 5 – The Book Girl's Deduction

How can I use S's weakness?
How can I move S's heart and drag out all of its secrets?

I turned the problem over incessantly, but I stumbled upon the key to destroying S when I wasn't even looking.

⟫•◆•⟪

I spent the last weekend of May in a funk.

Even when I was playing video games in my room, or watching a DVD, or playing with my little sister, or eating with my family, I couldn't forget Takeda's desolate look or her declaration that "Someone like you...could never understand!" It blurred into another person's face and voice and sent me into a lingering depression.

I was playing a card game in the living room with Maika, who had just started elementary school that year, when my mother brought in our dinner. She asked me, "Konoha looks sad, doesn't he? Did something happen at school?"

"Huh? No, nothing. It's the same as always."

"Really?"

"Come on, I swear it's nothing."

My mom smiled faintly.

"I suppose. You've been much more cheerful since you started high school, like you used to be. I'm glad that you seem to be enjoying high school."

"Yeah, I'm having fun."

The last couple days hadn't been so great, but maybe tomorrow I'd be able to get back to my regular life.

Not arguing, not struggling, not clinging to wild hopes; just peaceful and ordinary. I would go to book club after school and write snacks for Tohko until the setting sun filled the room with gold. I would listen to Tohko's litanies. I would needle her...

"All right, time for dinner. Go get your father, Maika."

"'Kay."

Maika scampered off. My mother picked up again in a gentle voice. "Konoha, as long as you're happy, that's all we want for you."

"Thanks, Mom."

Two years ago, I put my family through a lot.

The trade-off for my unearned glory was losing something that I valued and adored for a very long time.

I didn't want to do that ever again.

After dinner, I collapsed into bed and listened to my favorite music on my headphones. Something fast and upbeat to cheer me up.

While I was listening to it, I suddenly thought of Tohko.

I wonder what Tohko ate today.

I hadn't been writing snacks for her much lately.

When I told her about Takeda's boyfriend, she looked very sad.

I thought that finding out she'd been tricked, when she had gone so far as to strip in front of me in order to get information, was driving her toward tears, so I jokingly offered, "Come on, don't look so sad. Want me to go squeeze that report out of her? She's all cuddly with that classmate of hers, so I bet she would write something sweet enough to give you a toothache. Just how you like it."

But Tohko shook her head and looked even sadder. "It's not that. You look closer to tears than I do."

My faculties failed me, and all I could do was fall silent.

First my mom, now Tohko—all I did was make people worry.

I felt pathetic and angry at myself.

"I'll write you something sweet tomorrow, Tohko."

———◈———

Like poison falling—*drip, drip*—I watched with naked awareness on my face as—little by little—S went insane.

I can tell that S's usual ease has disappeared.

And that S's eyes are roving skittishly, and that S's voice is quavering.

Now and then, S has begun to sigh when no one is around and to tear at their hair, and to spin around to look over their shoulder in surprise.

Very soon.

My preparations are complete.

All that remains is to turn the key and open the door.

I have written a letter to S.

I'm waiting on the roof.

Let's discuss the truth.

The next day, too, the weather was beautiful.

From the classroom window, I could see the sky was a bright, translucent blue, and the new leaves glimmered in the sunlight. During one of the breaks between classes, I hung my head out the window and filled my lungs with the air of early summer.

I sat back down and noticed Akutagawa coming toward me. It was rare for the taciturn Akutagawa to seek out a conversation with anyone.

"The alumni came again on Friday. They were asking about you."

"Huh? What about?"

"What class you're in, what sort of guy you are."

They were probably wondering about me because I looked like Shuji. Now that I knew Shuji had committed suicide, I also understood why they'd been at such a loss when I questioned them before.

"I'll let them know the main stuff."

"Thanks, Akutagawa."

He nodded and went back to his seat.

I remembered that I had to return Kotobuki's ten yen to her, and dug around for my wallet.

Great, I actually have it today.

I went over to Kotobuki and held the coin out to her. "Here's your change."

Kotobuki bit her lip nervously and looked away from me. "…Thanks."

"Thanks for replacing the book for me. Later."

"Uh, hey…"

"Hm?"

She hesitated, then muttered a sullen "Nothing" and fell silent. Maybe she was still thinking about how she'd told me that Takeda had a boyfriend. I thought I probably ought to say something, but I knew that if I said anything wrong it would just rub her the wrong way, so I dropped the ten yen into Kotobuki's hand and went back to my seat.

When classes ended, I was walking down the hall to get to book club when I heard someone call my name behind me.

When I turned to look, I was surprised to see who was standing there, panting.

"Is something wrong?"

"There's something important I need to talk to you about. Would you come with me?"

"Huh? But—"

"It won't take long. Please. It's urgent."

"... All right."

I followed helplessly where he led.

Why had he come looking for me? Had something happened? He looked tense and forbidding.

He climbed farther and farther up the stairs.

Third floor—

Fourth floor—

He pressed on in silence but for the clicking of his footsteps, his eyes fixed intently ahead.

When I realized where he was going, I felt a chill.

"Um, where are we going?"

"The roof."

Fear gripped my heart and a wave of numbness assaulted me, tingling through my lips and fingertips.

An image flashed into my mind: a sky like the deep blue ocean above, concrete below, heat rising up in shimmering waves, my shadow and the girl's, the water tank, the rusty guard-rails...

The girl stopping in front of the rails and turning around—

"I'm sorry, I *can't* go on the roof."

The numbness in my fingers grew stronger, and my misgivings rapidly deepened. My legs crumpled with terror to the point where I thought I might fall to my knees, but the man yanked me up harshly by the arm.

Pain shot through my arm. I thought it was funny that the pain jolted my thoughts out of the past and back to the present.

"We can't talk with other people around. It'll be quick, I swear."

He stared down at me, his eyes as glassy as those of a dead fish. There was something odd in his voice, and I realized in that moment just how great and frightening was the threat that had hold of me.

"Not the roof—"

"What are you afraid of? What's wrong with the roof?" He jerked on my arm as he spoke, his voice trembling. "After all, you wanted to talk to me about something, too, didn't you?"

"Please let go of me. *I don't want to go on the roof!*"

The man gripped my arm with terrifying strength and pulled open the door to the roof with his other hand.

I felt wind pelt my face.

It had been windy that day, too. She turned around when she reached the rails and a gentle summer breeze played through her hair and across her skirt.

No!

No!

Stop—

The man dragged me out to the middle of the roof despite my thrashing and shouted, "You sent me a letter!"

What was this guy talking about? Did I write a letter? Was he talking about the love letters I'd written for Takeda?

Fear from both past and present mingled, making my fingers ache and my breath come in short, painful bursts. My head felt like it was being pounded from every direction at once. Cold sweat broke out on my forehead and dripped into my eyes, clouding my vision.

Unable to draw a full breath, I gulped down quick gasps of air. It was happening again. I had forgotten about it all this time.

"You sent me a letter! *Didn't you*, Shuji?"

I felt him grab the collar of my uniform. He pushed his twisted face closer to mine.

"No, Soeda! I'm not Shuji Kataoka!"

"Then why did you keep looking at me?" Soeda bellowed. "With those mournful eyes that told me you knew everything?"

When I'd first seen him at the archery team, he struck me as placid and intellectual. This total reversal inspired a depthless terror in me.

Who was this person? Was this really the same man?

"You were always—always!—looking at me! Even after Sakiko died! Never saying a word, just looking at me! That's how you punished me for killing her!"

Alternating between hyperventilation and asphyxiation, I croaked out a question.

"I thought—Sakiko—died—in an—accident?"

Soeda's eyes were shot through with his pulsing blood. He spat back, "So innocent! And after you told us you were staying late for club business, after you asked me to take her home. After you

said, 'I'm trusting you with my girlfriend,' with that unguarded, ever-present smile of yours.

"I was the one who liked her first. You knew how I felt, but you seduced her anyway. You made her fall in love with you and then you started dating. Then you dared to tell me that she had begged to go out with you. What else could you do, right?

"You were always like that! Irresponsible, blowing everything off, always joking around—but you still had to come up behind me and swipe the things I wanted. You would have overtaken me in archery by the end, and the girls I liked always wound up falling for you.

"I hated you for that, more than I can even bear to think about. I struggled to keep it from showing on my face; but you just watched me keep my cool with a little smirk.

"I loathed that caring look you could assume—and how you smiled!

"'I'm trusting you with my girlfriend now'—how could you say that? If it weren't for you, she would have been going out with me! But you have the nerve to tell me, 'I'm trusting you with my girlfriend now'?

"You knew how I felt about her. You were so sure that I could never win her over. You were mocking me!"

Soeda tightened his grip on my collar, and it dug into my neck.

Soeda's face swirled through my mind, clouding my thoughts, as images of Shuji Kataoka and Miu, the girl I'd seen for the last time on the roof, rose up beside him.

Hey, how come you never talk to me? Are you ignoring me? Do I look like I'm in that much pain?

When I followed her up to the roof, Miu had smiled at me sadly.

—*Konoha, I don't think you would ever understand.*

*　　*　　*

"You could never understand what I've been through! I told Sakiko how I felt about her that day and begged her to break up with you. She pushed past me and ran away—she ignored the traffic light and tried to cross the road just to get away from me. That was when the truck hit her. When she died. I got scared and I ran; I was a coward.

"If I—if I hadn't said anything…If it weren't for *you*, that never would have happened! I never would have killed her or acted like a coward.

"You never talked to me about her after that. Even though you knew that I should have been with her when it happened. You just looked at me silently and never questioned me about it.

"That was how you got your fun tormenting me!"

Whistling sounds escaped my constricted throat. I couldn't catch my breath. My fingertips were trembling and numb.

No! Shuji wasn't enjoying it! He was always alone, always in pain.

I wanted to tell him that, but I couldn't speak.

Soeda's face twisted in anguish, and his grip tightened around my throat.

"I brought a knife up to this very roof that day, and I stabbed you. I don't remember if you tried to call for help. You walked over to the railing and threw yourself over. So *why*? Why are you here *now*? I'm going to have a child next year! I just want to forget about you and live my life. Why do you haunt me? You've lived in my thoughts these ten long years! And now you've reappeared! Why? Why won't you let me be free? I'm going to have a child! I thought I would finally be able to relax. As long as you live, I will kill you! As many times as it takes!"

The collar of my shirt bit into my neck. Soeda's fingers were shaking.

117

A kaleidoscope of images flashed through my mind.

Miu poking her head out in front of me to look up at me teasingly. Her sweet smell of shampoo mixed with sweat.

The serene smile Shuji Kataoka wore in his picture.

Miu bent over a pile of paper, focused on a story she was writing during class. And myself, gazing at her slender back adoringly.

Soeda's face, twisted in pain; Shuji's face; Miu's face.

Soeda, stabbing Shuji. Shuji, falling to his death. Miu, turning to look back at me in front of the railing.

Konoha, I don't think you would ever understand.

You would never understand.

You would never understand.

Still looking straight at me, Miu's body arched slowly backward and over the railing.

A line from *No Longer Human* came to mind.

The woman died.

The woman died.

Maybe I'll die, too.

Just then, I felt a body strike mine.

"You let go of Konoha!"

Takeda forced her tiny body between me and Soeda, shoving him away.

My legs crumpled, and I fell into a sitting position, but Takeda helped me back up.

"Konoha, are you okay? Konoha!"

Breathing wildly, I managed a quiet, "Takeda..."

Takeda's face was pinched, on the verge of tears. She gently helped me lie down on the concrete, then turned to face Soeda with a harsh look. "I knew you were the one who killed Shuji. *You were S, weren't you, Mister Soeda?*"

"Who are you...?"

"Chia Takeda, a first-year student. I wrote you that letter in Shuji's name. And I'm the one who told you to come to the roof today."

"You *what?*"

Soeda's mouth dropped open.

"Why would you do that?"

"Because I wanted to know who S was. Because he was with Shuji at the very end."

I heard a rustling noise. Takeda had pulled a folded-up letter from her pocket and was showing it to Soeda.

"Shuji left a second suicide note—the real one—besides the one he left at his house. It was inside a book in a basement storage room. It had been withdrawn from the library and gone unnoticed by anyone for ten whole years. I found it.

"Shuji knew that S was involved in the death of his girlfriend. But the reason he never said anything was because he'd sent her with S on purpose, to test her. It led to Sakiko's death.

"He confesses in this letter. 'I killed her. I tested her faithfulness out of some dark emotion, and I watched her die.' So he thought he deserved to die, and he wanted S to kill him!"

Takeda read from a part of a letter that Tohko and I had never seen, her voice as bleak as a storm gusting through dead branches.

"'S is cornered.

"'It was S's scheme which led to Sakiko's death. S knows the stain of that crime can never be erased and fears being implicated in it.

"'I treated S as I always have. I look at S and even smile. I'm watching closely as S's mind twists, little by little, as it creaks and screams.

119

" 'I've seen S's murderous impulse, finding no other outlet, turn toward me—I've prayed that S would kill me.

" 'That will be my atonement.

" 'S is my enemy, my friend, and the person who best understands me. So I'm sure S has realized my intentions. I pray that S will send me from this world.' The letter ends when Shuji calls S up to the roof."

It was the second letter.

There was another installment to the first letter, after all.

Takeda had only shown us the first part.

"After I read this letter, I talked to some of the teachers and looked some stuff up, and I found out that Shuji Kataoka had been a student here and that ten years ago he'd committed suicide up here. I wondered if it had really been suicide, or if maybe S had killed him. That was the day that Shuji was supposed to meet S on the roof. S knew the truth. I needed to know it, too.

"And since *you* are S, Mister Soeda, I sent letters to you signed as Shuji. Because when you saw Konoha, who looks exactly like Shuji, you were the calmest one. I thought your reaction was unnatural. And you never looked at Konoha again, did you? Mister Manabe was so disturbed that he couldn't stop looking at Konoha. But you kept your eyes away because you didn't want to risk seeing him. So I kept sending you letters under Shuji's name, about things only Shuji and S would know. Please tell me—what did you and Shuji say to each other that day on the roof?"

"Say?" Soeda mumbled, his voice now depleted of all its force. "We didn't say anything. I stabbed him, he got stabbed without saying a word, and then it was over."

"No—" Takeda's voice was tinged with despair.

"He can't answer your question. That's not S."

120

*   *   *

I craned my neck as far as it would go to look toward the voice.

I saw a thin figure standing perfectly straight. Black bangs swept over a pale forehead. Two long braids danced in the wind like cats' tails. She had a clear, intelligent gaze.

My vision was clouded by sweat, but Tohko's shape as she stood in the doorway to the stairwell was starkly, vividly familiar.

My heart swelled instantly. I thought I might cry.

Takeda—

Soeda—

They stared at Tohko in surprise.

"W-who are you?" Soeda asked, his voice trembling.

Tohko's stalwart answer was, "I'm the book girl."

Geez, what was she doing? This was serious.

I felt the last of my strength leave me and pressed my cheek to the warm, sunbathed concrete. Tohko never stopped being Tohko.

"I am also the kind and charming club president to whom that boy on the ground over there turns for support."

Please don't speak for me... Soeda and Takeda didn't seem to know what to make of her, either.

Tohko stalked over to us, sending her long braids flying.

"Your wife and friend came looking for you at the book club, Mister Soeda."

Manabe and Rihoko appeared behind Tohko. Soeda paled at the sight of them, taken aback. "Rihoko...Manabe! What are you doing here?"

Rihoko looked down. "You've been acting strangely. Restless, as if you're afraid of something. And then today I found a stack of letters while I was cleaning your room. I was so surprised to

see that they were from Shuji Kataoka that I read them. I tried to call you at work, but they told me you'd left early. I started to worry."

"Rihoko called me and said she thought you might be coming here to see Konoha—or rather, Shuji. So you killed him, Soeda..." Manabe's voice was pained, too. "I knew you liked Sakiko. And I suspected that you had some sort of fixation on Shuji. But that you'd killed him? If I'd known that..."

Manabe looked at Rihoko and bit his lip, unable to go on.

Her eyes still downcast, Rihoko rested her hands tensely on her stomach.

His crime revealed to his wife and friend, the people closest to him, Soeda's face shuddered in despair.

"What choice did I have?" he pleaded. "There was no other way for me to find peace. I had to kill Shuji..."

Tohko spoke up once more in her lofty tone. "No, Soeda's not the one who killed Shuji. He isn't S. It's someone else."

"That can't be!" Takeda countered. "When Soeda saw Konoha, he acted the most suspiciously. Besides, my letters had an effect on him!"

"You overlooked something very important, Chia. While it's true that S was Shuji's enemy, it was also the person who best understood him. I haven't read anything but the very beginning of the letter that you showed us, so I can only draw my conclusions from that. But Shuji writes again and again that S sees through everything, that S is the only one his clowning doesn't work on.

"So S can't be Mister Soeda.

"If he understood Shuji, he wouldn't have to hate him or have this obsession with him."

Takeda was flustered. "Then...who *is* S?"

"I'm not a detective from Baker Street or an old lady who solves crimes while she's knitting in an easy chair. I'm just a book girl. So I can't make a deduction, only take a flight of fancy—er, forget I said that. I meant, I can only take a guess.

"Shuji Kataoka was a huge fan of Osamu Dazai, and he left the record of his true feelings in a suicide note tucked inside a copy of *No Longer Human*. You can feel Dazai's influence on him throughout the letter. The opening line, 'Mine has been a life of shame,' is a direct quote. I think that Shuji must have read *No Longer Human* and seen himself in its protagonist, who 'cannot guess at the nature or degree of people's pain,' and who talks about his inability to 'give up on humanity, despite fearing it with all my being.' He can only attempt to win people's affection by playing the fool. I think Shuji must have identified with that very deeply.

"In *No Longer Human*, there are two characters, each of them totally unlike the other, who realize that the protagonist's clowning is only an act. One of them is the protagonist's classmate from middle school, a boy named Takeichi. He's described as a bad student who wears clothes that are too big for him, can't study, and always sits out of gym class. One day this unimpressive boy, who the protagonist never would have thought needed watching, points out that his disarming behavior is totally premeditated. This shocks the protagonist, who feels as if the fires of hell are burning the world to cinders around him. He decides to become friends with Takeichi so he can keep an eye on him.

"The other is the detective investigating the protagonist after he attempts double suicide and is the only survivor. He's an impressive man who gives off 'an air of enlightened calm and who anyone would call handsome.' He immediately sees

through the protagonist's act and gives him a look of quiet contempt, which allows the protagonist to taste the shame of a 'cold sweat.'"

Tohko expounded seamlessly on the roof of the school, her long braids streaming around her in the breeze. Something more compelling than usual animated her manner, and no one attempted to interrupt her revelations.

"S would neither have admired Shuji Kataoka nor hated him. It would be someone who saw Shuji with innocent, unsullied eyes, or someone who was able to observe him critically.

"It was someone Shuji was always with. Someone who watched Shuji, criticized him, and occasionally gave him advice.

"Rihoko—your maiden name was Sena, correct?"

Soeda's wife, Rihoko, started, then nodded, her face taut. "Yes, that's right."

"Ten years ago you were the manager for the archery team. I've heard that girls would flock around Shuji at team practices and the manager was always yelling at him for it. You were the only one Shuji never rebelled against.

"You're S, aren't you?"

Rihoko gasped. Her hands tightened against her stomach. Then she looked right back at Tohko. Her voice was hard with resolve when she spoke. "Yes. I'm S, and I killed both Shuji and Sakiko."

"Rihoko!"

"What are you saying, Rihoko?"

Manabe and Soeda cried out in the same instant.

Soeda ran to her side. "Don't be ridiculous! I stabbed Shuji! And Sakiko—I watched Sakiko get hit by the truck, watched her blood spill onto the road!"

125

"But I was the one who kept Kataoka back and made sure that you took Sakiko home. And don't you remember? When you told me how you felt about Sakiko, I only pretended to care and suggested that you force Sakiko to hear you out."

"You only—" Soeda's voice choked off.

"I was also the one who dared Kataoka to bet whether Sakiko would switch to Soeda. Kataoka took the bet and sent Sakiko home with him—with you, dear. Then Kataoka and I followed the two of you in secret."

"No... Then when Sakiko was killed, you two were—"

"Yes. We saw it happen. We saw her body leap into the air, saw it strike the ground, saw you run away—everything."

Soeda was struck utterly speechless.

Manabe turned on Rihoko in his place. "Why would you do something like that, Rihoko? I thought you hated Shuji for being such a slacker. And besides, back then we were—"

"Yes, we were dating back then. You were confident and straightforward, which was very charming. I liked you very much.

"In contrast, Kataoka was a slacker who did nothing but tell stupid jokes. He didn't seem to even try to be serious with anyone, so I hated him.

"But then one day I was so annoyed I told him, 'Not a single thing you say is true. You're just acting, trying to fool all of us.' He was so surprised, he looked like he might start crying. He looked so vulnerable and sad that I couldn't stay away."

Manabe fell into the same silence that had claimed Soeda.

Tohko murmured, "So you became his confidante, and then you fell in love with him."

"Yes. After that, I was the only one Kataoka didn't try to deceive. I was the only one he confided his pain and sadness to. Do you think a girl could help but love someone like Kataoka when he surrendered his heart to her entirely?"

126

A sad look crossed Tohko's face. "No."

Rihoko smirked. "Kataoka was sneaky and impossible and childish. But he was a kind, complicated person. He was someone you couldn't help liking."

"How odd. Do you know Tomie Yamazaki, the woman who committed double suicide with Osamu Dazai in the Tama River? She kept a diary, and in it, she said that Dazai was sneaky. But she loved him anyway. She said he was the sort of person you couldn't help liking."

"Yeah. Kataoka loved *No Longer Human*. He read it so many times, his copy was falling apart. Even though he told Sakiko that he never read books because it made him sleepy.

"Kataoka was going out with Sakiko, but she knew nothing about him. That began to burden Kataoka eventually. So I manipulated Soeda into trying to separate them.

"Maybe I was just jealous of her.

"Because of my simpleminded plot, Sakiko was killed, and the guilt utterly destroyed the already delicate balance of Kataoka's psyche. He began to wish only for death.

"He never blamed me for what happened to Sakiko. I wish he would have, but he only looked at me in silence. Every time I saw the words 'please kill me' written on his face, I felt trapped.

"I could never have killed him.

"But he wished for death.

"He'd always wanted to die, but now he desired it with all his heart. Now he was convinced that death was the only way he could escape his suffering.

"What should I have done? Maybe granting his wish would have been proof of my love for him.

"A month after Sakiko's death, I found a letter from Kataoka in my desk at school. He was asking me to meet him on the roof so we could have an honest discussion. I knew the time had finally

come when I would have to make up my mind. The world seemed bleak.

"I didn't want to go.

"I wanted to blow it off and go home. I thought maybe Kataoka would give up those dangerous ideas if he had to wait up there for nothing.

"But then—what if Kataoka died alone? What if he lost all hope when I didn't come and latched on to his darkest, most pitiful feelings and threw himself off the roof?

"Once I started thinking like that, I couldn't stand it. Of course I had to go."

"So Shuji was still alive when you got to the roof."

Rihoko nodded.

"On my way up the stairs, I saw Soeda running down looking pale. When I went out onto the roof, Kataoka was sitting limply on the ground with a knife sticking out of his chest. He looked at me, his expression somewhere between laughing and crying, and he murmured, 'This isn't going to kill me...A shallow wound like this is never going to stop my heart.'"

Takeda had listened to everything in silence, but now a question broke from her in a groan. "What happened next?"

"He...asked me to kill him. He begged me. 'I'm tired,' he said. 'Please, just kill me.'"

Everyone gasped.

Rihoko's voice shook, like the hands which still cradled her belly.

"Kataoka staggered to his feet and asked to borrow my handkerchief. When I handed it to him, he wiped away the fingerprints on the knife and gave it back to me. Then he staggered toward the railing."

I could see Shuji Kataoka ever so slowly approaching the railing.

The image of Miu obscured it.

I knew—I had witnessed a similar scene of despair.

Ever so slowly, Miu will walk toward her death.

The wind will play across the skirt of her uniform, and she'll turn around.

"He turned around and looked at me. His eyes were so empty."

Miu's eyes had been forlorn, and terribly bright.

"'You're the only one who can kill me, Sena. Even now, I still don't understand why people feel the way they do. I have no idea why Soeda hated me so much that he had to stab me. I can't feel even a little bit sad about Sakiko dying right in front of me. I remember something Dazai wrote: 'I want to die, I ought to die, I cannot undo what I have done, no matter what I do, everything I do, it turns out wrong, it only adds another layer of shame.' I wonder what he was thinking when he wrote that. I feel like I'm standing right next to him. I understand how he feels. Is there any value in a life like mine? I know you can answer that, Sena. Please tell me.'"

Miu had said, *Konoha, I don't think you would ever understand.*

"I couldn't save Kataoka.

"If I loved him, I had to grant him his last wish.

"So I told him what he wanted to hear.

"I said, 'No, you're no longer human.'"

I hadn't been able to say anything.

I couldn't speak, I couldn't move, I couldn't understand a word of what Miu was telling me.

"Kataoka smiled kindly.

"Like he was thanking me.

"Then he jumped off the roof.

"Osamu Dazai and I killed him."

Miu had smiled sadly and fallen off the roof.

I hadn't been able to do anything.

I watched her *die*...

"Stop!"

When I heard a voice cut through the air, I thought it was my own.

But it was Soeda. He had fallen to his knees on the concrete and was sobbing and holding his head.

"Please stop. I can't listen to this. It would have been better if I *had* killed him. You loved him? So then what does that make me? Why did you marry me, Rihoko?"

Rihoko answered quietly, "Because we were partners in crime. That's why I—I couldn't be with Manabe."

Manabe bit down on his lip, his face taut.

Rihoko kneeled down next to Soeda and hugged him, whispering, "Look, Soeda. You still hate Kataoka, still think about him, even now. You won't be able to forget him as long as you live, will you? Neither will I. I've never forgotten about him for a single day, either. And I never will forget about him. I'll always remember.

"Let's just accept it. We're prisoners to the same person, Soeda. We're partners in the same crime."

"We're—we're going to have a child! And now...How am I supposed to live with you now? It would be hell."

He pressed his hands over his face but couldn't stop the tears that fell, leaving small stains on the concrete.

Takeda watched him, her every ounce of strength drained away.

"Yes. We will live the rest of our lives in hell. It's not so bad: as long as you're prepared for it, you can live anywhere.

"Besides, I'm the only person in the entire world who won't

blame you for what you did to Kataoka. I don't think you were a coward, either, or that you were wretched or pathetic. In fact, I love you. If you think of it like that, you feel better, don't you?

"Come on, Yasuyuki. We'll go on with our peaceful, everyday lives, forever thinking about Kataoka, forever his prisoners. That will be our atonement to him."

Soeda's sobs echoed across the roof.

Tohko, Takeda, and Manabe were all silent.

And I...How could I possibly atone?

How could I be healed, how could I be saved?

Miu...Answer me, Miu!

"Konoha!"

Tohko was calling out to me.

I heard her footsteps running over to me, saw her braids falling over my face, felt her hugging me, smelled the fragrance of violets...

And then it was over.

In a cloud of overwhelming pain, I let go my hold on consciousness.

I first met Tohko a year ago.

It was an early afternoon in April, when the weather had just begun to thaw into warmth again after a winter of record-breaking tenacity.

The world's interest in Miu Inoue had faded, and I had finally been freed from the shadow of the cute little genius author. As a result, I had become a little lethargic. The wounds from what had happened on the roof had not yet healed.

Even after starting high school, I spent my time at lunch and after school in the schoolyard staring blankly at flowers and trees rather than trying to make friends or joining clubs.

One day after school while I was wandering around the grounds, I saw a girl with braids that hung down to her hips sitting under a white magnolia tree. She was leaning against the trunk and reading a book.

She had long eyelashes, and her skin was whiter than the magnolia flowers. The air seemed particularly tranquil where she was.

You don't see braids like that very much anymore. She looks like a girl from the 1900s. But she looks so mature. She must be an upperclassman...

I was captivated by her, lost in thoughts like these when...she tore a page out of the book.

Before my shock had time to register, she'd stuffed the page into her mouth.

What the—?

I watched her start to chew on it in even greater wonder; I felt like I was in a dream when suddenly she looked up at me.

Our eyes met, and I thought my heart would stop.

A blush popped into her cheeks, and when she spoke her voice was meek. "You saw that, didn't you?"

"Uh, well...that is...I'm sorry!"

"What's your name? What class are you in?"

"I'm Konoha Inoue, first year, third class."

She grinned at that, making her face look suddenly childlike. "I see...A first-year student? Then you need to join the book club."

"Wha—? The book club?"

I blinked at her in shock, and the strange girl with the long

braids—with the pure-white skin—with the clear, black eyes—with the book she had just taken a bite of—said, "I'm going to keep you nearby so you don't spill my secret. From this day forward, you are a member of the book club."

"*What?* H-hold on a second! I—I can't be in the...Who are you anyway?"

"I am Tohko Amano, in class eight of the second-years. As you can see, I am a book girl."

That was how we met.

During the next month, Tohko would come to my classroom after school and say, "All right, Konoha, it's time for a club meeting," as if she were a class monitor coming to collect a classmate who didn't want to go to school. Then she would drag me by the hand to the room on the western corner of the third floor where the book club met.

When we got to the room, she would hand me a packet of paper stapled into a notebook and ask, "Do you know what improv stories are? It's when a storyteller takes three prompts from an audience and makes up an unscripted performance. I'm going to give you three words, and I want you to try writing something, whether it's a poem, an essay, a fairy tale, or whatever. Hmm... let's see...let's try clouds, green tea shortbread, and ant bundles. You have fifty minutes. Okay, go!"

"What are ant bundles?"

"Better get started, or I'll put a curse on you."

Every day she did that and made me write I-don't-even-know-what.

"I eat stories instead of bread or rice. I usually eat books, but I love handwriting the best. Love stories are sugary, so I like those even better. So you better write me a *suuuuper* yummy story."

133

Familiarity is a frightening thing, because eventually I accepted her explanation as something ordinary.

But since she would crunch through the things I wrote with a mouthful of criticism—*"Nom-nom...* this one tastes a little watered-down," or *"Mmf-mmf...* the structure is still a little raw"—what could I do but accept it?

Before I realized it, I started going to the book club after school even when Tohko didn't come for me.

"You seem much happier lately, Konoha. Did something nice happen at school?"

"It...it's nothing like that! Everything's the same as usual!"

Some doubt remained whether spending my days with an upperclassman who tore the pages out of books and ate them could be called in any way normal, but whenever I went to book club, where tiny motes of dust floated through the beams of the setting sun, I felt strangely at ease. Though I was flabbergasted by the things Tohko said and did, I started to have fun making the occasional wry comment, and I didn't have to force myself to smile around her.

I went to book club every single day.

"Hello, Konoha."

"I'm sooo hungryyy, Konoha."

"Wow, your story today was so sweet! You're getting good, Konoha!"

"You know, I really think you could stand to be a little more respectful of your elders, Konoha."

"I am *not* a goblin! I'm just a book girl!"

Every day I talked to Tohko, wrote snacks for Tohko, saw Tohko smile, and so I started to think about Miu less.

So I guess it serves me right.

I'm sorry, Miu. I am.

I didn't forget about you. It's just that it hurt so much to remember you.

Every story you wrote was so gentle and warm and shining, and when you were talking about your dreams, you were dazzling. I adored you.

So I still don't understand why you threw yourself off the roof that day.

I can never write again.

Because they're all lies. Because I'm totally empty.

Miu Inoue doesn't exist.

I can never write again. I won't. I don't want to.

When I woke up, someone was holding my hand softly.

I saw a white roof, white walls. The sheets smelled of medicine.

"Is this... the hospital?"

"No, you're in the nurse's office," Tohko answered. "You passed out on the roof. Mister Manabe carried you down here. I tried to pick you up myself, though, really! I put your arm over my shoulders, but when I tried to lift you, I landed flat on my butt. Manual labor really is impossible for a scholar."

Tohko was seated on a chair at my bedside, gently holding my hand.

Orange light cut through a gap in the curtains.

"How long was I out?"

"Two hours, maybe? You were sweating a lot. And moaning."

Had she been holding my hand that whole time?

"What happened to everyone else?"

"Soeda went back home with Rihoko. I think they're going to

135

stay together, loving and hating Shuji for the rest of their lives...
They've passed judgment on themselves."

I remembered how Soeda had sobbed that his life would
be hell.

I wondered if they would stay together as a family.

Tohko stroked the back of my hand softly with a finger.
Gently...gently...It was like she was comforting me.

"Mister Manabe and Chia went home, too. Chia told me to tell
you that she's very sorry for getting you involved."

"I guess the only reason Takeda took me to see the archery
team was so those alums could get a look at me. She only got
closer to me because I look so much like Shuji."

"Yeah..." Tohko trailed off sadly.

Something hot surged up in me, and my throat trembled.

Takeda had used me.

Every letter I had written had been for nothing.

Takeda, Soeda, Rihoko, Shuji—all of them had lied. They'd
hidden the truth.

It would have been so much better if they'd just kept on lying
until the very end, so why had they started telling the truth?

They'd forced an impossible reality on me.

I had bundled my heart up in layer upon layer of soft cloth
in order to protect it, and they'd ripped it out of its hiding
spot, forcing it to bear first grief, then pain, misery, regret, and
desolation.

I didn't know how to deal with such a flood of emotions; there
was nothing I *could* do with them. My throat hurt, it burned, I
felt like my entire body had been dipped in flame, stinging...

I slipped my hand out of Tohko's, turned to stare up at the ceiling, and covered my face.

Otherwise she would see me crying.

"I'm so tired of watching these...messed up, irresponsible

things happen. I'm sick of it. I don't want drama or adventure or mysteries in my life. I'm tired of hurting and being sad and suffering.

"So why do people keep stirring up stuff they ought to just keep shut up inside themselves when they know it's going to hurt people? Do they want to know that badly? Do they have to lay everything out like that? Do they have to be so sad and suffer so much? Do they have to resent and hate people? Do they have to kill, and die?

"They're all...they're all crazy! It's not normal. I hate Osamu Dazai!"

Tears slid down my cheeks, wetting my ears, the collar of my shirt, and the sheets.

I felt a chill on the back of my neck.

I didn't get it. None of it.

Shuji and Miu both gave up on life and jumped to their deaths.

"*Nnk*...Such horrible things just keep happening...who knows what's normal and what's not anymore...I just don't get it, Tohko," I sobbed, surrounded by the smell of disinfectant in the room.

Tohko didn't try to say anything to comfort me. She only murmured sadly, "You have to find the answers to those questions on your own, Konoha. Even if it hurts...even if it makes you sad... even if you suffer along the way...you have to get there on your own."

"Then...*nnk*...I don't need to know. I'll just go on with my life without it."

I wonder how Tohko reacted to that.

The only difference between Tohko and me was that I was naïve enough to look for an answer.

Tohko wasn't a fortune-teller or a counselor or a psychologist.

She was a goblin who ate the written word, but that was the only thing that separated us. Because she was just a regular high school girl, just a regular book girl.

Tohko didn't say anything more.

She stayed with me in the nurse's office as the sun fell below the horizon and the room became cool and dark, until I stopped crying.

Chapter 6 – The Book Girl's Allegation

Several days went by.

After the incident on the roof, I never once spoke to Takeda, and she never came looking for me.

The day before, Kotobuki had said, "I haven't seen your girl lately. Did you two break up?"

I saw a little red along the tops of her cheeks, and she hung her head, fidgeting. Her voice almost sounded concerned.

"We were never going out in the first place. And she doesn't need my help anymore, so I don't think she's coming back."

"I—I didn't, I mean, it's not a big deal, I just thought...maybe I'd gone too far before. I mean...um..."

She looked up and as soon as our eyes met, she flushed an even darker red.

"N-never mind!"

She whirled around and walked away.

But just when I'd thought she was gone, she stopped in her tracks and circled back around, extremely agitated.

"That is, I—um...er...no, it's really nothing!" she stammered loudly, then hurried away.

She was probably trying to apologize. She could be harsh, but I guess she wasn't a bad person.

I went to book club every day and passed the time politely listening to Tohko as she expounded on her criticism of books while I wrote her improv stories.

"Today's topics are stapler, amusement park, and mutton hot pot. You have exactly fifty minutes. Okay, go!"

Bang!

Tohko started her silver stopwatch. She propped her elbows on the back of her fold-up chair and leaned forward. She kicked off her shoes and kneeled on the chair. Her manners were as bad as ever.

"What's mutton hot pot?"

"You haven't *heard* of it? It's mutton—so lamb would be okay, too—cut up into slices and then cooked really fast in soup. They did a story on a restaurant in Ginza on the news last night. They had such un-*believ*-ably thin cuts of meat for the soup. They said it didn't smell at all, and you could eat it raw and it would still melt on your tongue. The grape sherbet they had for dessert looked *so* yummy, too. After a hot meal, a cold dessert is really the only way to go. So I'd like a story that melts like lamb fillets for mutton hot pot and is chilly and sweet like ice cream."

"You need to stop ordering all this bizarre stuff. I mean, how can you be so easily influenced by TV and magazines and whatever else? How am I supposed to tie together a stapler, an amusement park, and lamb filets?"

"*That* is how the *chef* shows his skill. Heh-heh. I'm looking forward to this."

"Why don't you write something yourself for once?"

Tohko's index finger popped up immediately and her face turned serious. "Konoha, as your mentor, allow me to teach you something about life."

"That being?"

"Food that someone else makes for you tastes ten times better than your own cooking."

"You're avoiding the question."

"And also? Food cooked with affection is a hundred times better. That's also a fact."

She rested her chin on her hand, leaning on the back of her chair, and beamed at me as if she could compel me to write this story with a huge helping of affection.

I got it: a sheep with staplers sticking out of it like a hedgehog gets lost in an amusement park and gets tricked by a witch, who makes him into a mutton hot pot.

Tohko watched me idly as my pen raced across the pages of the notebook.

"It's hard to write with you watching me. Could you read a book or something?"

"Sure thing, chef."

She spun around in her chair and started reading one of the old books in the room, dangling her legs over the edge of the chair.

After a while, the only noises in the cramped room were the scratching of my pen on the paper and the rustling of pages being turned in Tohko's book, mingling with the dust motes suspended in the air.

Without warning, her back still turned to me, Tohko murmured, "Hey, Konoha. How do you think little Chia is doing?"

My pen paused momentarily.

I didn't want Tohko to think I was shaken, so I quickly resumed writing.

"I dunno...does it matter anymore?"

"But she still hasn't turned in her report."

Tohko turned back around to look at me. "Konoha, would you go and talk to her and get the report?"

I gaped. "Do you hear yourself talking? No. I don't want to."

"But, but, but, but—she promised she would write a report for me when the contract was finished."

"You'd be sick for a week if you ate a report about what happened. I won't do it! Absolutely not! If you want to eat weird stuff like that, why don't you go and get it yourself?"

Tohko looked sad.

Uh-oh. Had I gone too far?

"Konoha, little Chia may have lied to you, but wasn't there some truth to what she said after all?

"You haven't asked her why she did it. Are you going to let it end without knowing? You wrote all those love letters because you wanted to help Chia out, right?"

I said nothing, just pressed on with the story.

"Done."

I tore three sheets of paper out of the packet and handed them to Tohko.

"Be sure to clean your plate."

My story about the sheep covered in staplers who gets filleted must have tasted pretty unusual. Tohko struggled to choke down the three sheets of paper, and there were tears in her eyes.

"Urf, gross…no I mean, that really spoke to me. The taste is v-very unique and th-this part…*it's so gross*…n-no, delicious. It's delicious…really. Urg…if I tell myself it's good, it'll taste good…bleh."

She was such a lost cause.

She'd eaten entire stories as nonsensical as that and with worse editing before.

She'd done the same thing when I had first joined the book club last year.

She would try her very best to eat the grotesque stories that I

wrote badly on purpose, without a single punctuation mark and my subjects and objects every which way. Then she would correct my errors with ridiculous gravity.

"That was good, but...I like punctuation because it shows you when to take a breath when you're telling a story. If there's too much of it, that can mess up the flow, too, but for now why don't you try it out? And maybe you shouldn't use the exact same sentence structure quite so much."

No matter how often I slapped together something weird to be mean, Tohko would eat it all, and the next day she would come pick me up with a smile and say, "Time for the club meeting, Konoha!"

Maybe it was because I was still inside my shell back then and avoided interacting with people, so she didn't feel like she could just abandon me.

She often struck me as unfiltered and self-absorbed, an utterly carefree book girl living in her own world who cared not at all about the world around her. But Tohko could also be a busybody.

Maybe being with Tohko for a whole year had had an effect on me.

The next day I headed to the library to see Takeda.

"I don't care what her reasons were for tricking me. Tohko is a pig, and now she wants to eat Takeda's report, so I'm just here to collect it," I reminded myself as I spiraled down the rusty staircase to the basement storage room.

Clang-clang-clang.

The noise of my footsteps was swallowed up in the underground stillness.

Descending the final step, I went to the door at the end of the corridor and knocked. A cautious voice responded, "Er, yes?"

"It's Inoue, from the literature club."

"Konoha! J-just a second!"

Beyond the door, I heard the sound of books toppling over and being tossed aside, a mouse squeaking, a voice saying, "Shh! Go away!" to chase it off, then a brief silence before the door opened and Takeda appeared, looking sheepish. "Um…c-come in. The mice are gone so…it's safe."

"…Thanks."

The storage room was the same as the last time I'd been there, with the sweet smell of old paper in the air, dingy with dust.

The lamp that stood on the school desk gave off a faint illumination, like a streetlight casting its isolated glow into the darkness. An orange thermos sat on top of the desk alongside a box of cookies and a mug with a drawing of a duck on it.

"Tohko told me to come and ask you when your report is going to be ready."

Takeda lowered her eyes. "I'm sorry. I made a draft, but then I reread it and…it was totally unusable…I guess I have no writing ability after all."

Not knowing how to respond, I said nothing. Takeda kept her face down and made herself even smaller.

"I really am sorry that I lied to you and Tohko. I—I wanted to be a detective. My life was so ordinary and boring. I thought it might make it more interesting if I had a boyfriend, so I started dating Hiro, and I really liked him a lot so I tried to be satisfied with that, but…the duck never changed into a princess. It was fun at first, but after I got used to it, I felt like, oh…this is all it is.

"That's when I found Shuji's letter.

"My heart ached so badly while I was reading it, I just started to cry.

"It was like the world had changed color.

"I wanted to find out more about him.

"I wanted to get closer to him.

"I thought I might be able to become someone different than who I'd always been. Maybe even a girl like me could be part of a wonderful story that was full of thrills and excitement.

"That's…what I thought."

"You're the one who cut his picture out of the yearbook, aren't you?"

"Yes. While I was researching Shuji, it started getting more and more important to me to know whether or not he'd really committed suicide…

"I would hole up in this room after school and make up all kinds of theories. It was a lot of fun. I felt like I'd become a detective for real.

"I should have left it at that.

"When I saw you handing out flyers at the school entrance, I—you looked so much like Shuji that I almost forgot to breathe.

"That's when I realized that if I could have you meet the old archery club members, I'd be able to tell who S was and then I could learn the truth about Shuji's death."

So Takeda had used the relationship advice box that Tohko set up as an excuse to get close to me so she could achieve her own goals.

Shuji does *too* exist! Really!

Takeda had sworn it to me again and again.

For her, Shuji Kataoka was not merely a phantom known only through his letters: he was a real flesh-and-blood human being.

She'd wanted to believe that.

That was how powerful a role Shuji had played for her.

But now Takeda seemed bereft.

"My stupid ideas put you through a lot of trouble, and I'm sorry. Even now that I know the truth, my heart still hurts and nothing's changed."

Takeda picked up her mug with the drawing of the duck on it. "My best friend, the one who gave me this cup, died two years ago in an accident. She was hit by a car, just like Sakiko."

So that's what it was.

Maybe the reason Takeda had been so obsessed with Shuji was because, like him, she'd lost someone she cared about in a traffic accident. I felt like I could understand that a little better, and my heart ached for her.

"She was strong and smart and optimistic, and she was our class monitor. She would have lived a much more spectacular life than someone like me will," Takeda murmured, her voice cracking.

Sorrow colored her eyes as she gazed at the mug.

"Takeda...I don't think there's anything wrong with being ordinary. I, at least, prefer it that way."

"I suppose..."

Takeda smiled sadly.

Then she looked up and said in a suddenly cheerful tone, "Did you know that today is the tenth anniversary of Shuji's death? So I've just been...enjoying a few last memories of him. But I have to get going. I'm meeting up with Hiro."

Takeda started gathering up the things on the desk.

She was smiling brightly, but there were tears rising in her eyes. She kept her eyes open as wide as possible to stop the tears from falling, and occasionally she would blink rapidly.

When she'd gotten her things together, Takeda smiled at me.

"I'm going to go. I'm really glad I got to talk to you, Konoha. Thank you for coming to see me."

"Takeda...you don't need to force yourself to write that report. I'm sure it's not very pleasant work, and I don't think writing it down will change anything."

A frail look passed over Takeda's face for a moment, then she

blinked again and tilted her head back slightly. When she looked back at me, the corners of her mouth were pulled up.

"You're right. I'll only feel miserable if I write about it. It's not going to change anything."

Even though I'd spoken the words myself, they cut into my heart when she repeated them.

No, writing doesn't change anything.

Writing won't save anybody.

Takeda murmured a good-bye, and the last smile she gave me was radiant.

Clang-clang-clang-clang…

I lingered in the sweet-smelling storage room and listened as Takeda's footsteps on the spiral staircase grew distant.

I remembered how she'd cried, clinging to me in the rain.

And I remembered her smile as she ate lunch with her boyfriend in the school yard.

Soeda and Rihoko had chosen to go on living together, never forgetting Shuji Kataoka.

But maybe Takeda had moved on.

Maybe she would spend her days in ordinary tranquillity with Hiro.

I believed she'd be happy that way.

All things pass.

Even Dazai said so in *No Longer Human*. Perhaps the passage of time is a kind of healing, or a kind of salvation granted equally to all people.

Feeling somewhat melancholy, I walked among the bookshelves, reading the titles of the volumes they contained.

Some titles I knew, some titles I didn't, some titles too worn to read: they all slipped by in the dim light of the room.

"Oh—"

But when I saw *that* title, I stopped. *"No Longer Human…"*

This might've been the book that Shuji put his letter in.

I hooked it with my finger and pulled it off the shelf. The book was inside a slipcover that had turned yellow, speckled with brown stains.

"Hm—it's stuck."

I couldn't get the book out.

"Maybe it's caught on something? Ack!"

I tugged harder and the book flew out of its case, along with a little notebook. They both landed on the floor and fell open.

When I bent over to pick them up, my heart skipped a beat.

There was a tiny photo on the floor that looked like it had been cut out of a larger picture. The boy in the picture looked back at me with my face.

A small notebook with a duck printed on the cover had fallen beside the photo.

This picture…was it from the yearbook? And wasn't this the notebook that Takeda was always carrying?

Why had she hidden it in a place like this? And why inside a copy of *No Longer Human*?

It was almost like—

I felt a terrible sense of foreboding.

I picked up the notebook and urgently scanned the narrow letters that packed each page.

As soon as I read the first line, I felt as if a pit were yawning open at my feet and I was going to topple headlong into it.

I read a bit more and then, unable to contain myself, flipped ahead to the last page. Cursing my stupidity, I shut the notebook and ran out of the room.

Mine has been a life of shame.

My grandmother's death was the first incident that showed me I was out of step with the rest of the world.

She'd been very fond of me. Even after an illness in her chest meant that she did little other than sleep, she wanted me by her side. She stroked my hair and called me "such a good girl, such a nice girl," her eyes crinkling with happiness.

But I wasn't the simple child my grandmother wished me to be. Her emaciated hands, her face guttered by wrinkles, her white, whispering husks of hair, her breath that reeked of medicine; all of it repelled and frightened me.

"You're a good girl, a nice girl."

Each time her croaking voice whispered in my ear, I felt as if she were putting a curse on me. My neck stiffened and goose bumps prickled my skin.

I was terrified that she would discover that I was not in fact a good girl; that as soon as my grandmother saw that in my heart I despised her, she would become a demon, her white hair bristling and her eyes burning red, and she would devour me. I would break into a cold, heavy sweat and some nights I found sleep impossible.

As I grew older, my impression that there was a significant disconnect between the way that I and other people experienced things only grew stronger. It took all the energy I had to summon even the slightest sympathy for things that made other people happy or sad.

Why does that make them happy?

Why does that make them sad?

When everyone was excited, cheering for their friends in sports competitions, when they were depressed at losing a friend who transferred to another school, I felt as uncomfortable as if I were in a room full of foreigners with whom I shared no common language. I flinched away from them and felt sharp pains in my stomach. The crushing din of words that everyone spoke around me was utterly incomprehensible.

Why? Why were they all crying? I just couldn't understand it. But it would be odd for one person to be unperturbed while the rest of them wept. I had to act like I was crying. My face was tense, so I couldn't cry very convincingly. My cheeks burned. What would I do if someone realized I was faking my tears? I just wouldn't lift my face. Hang your head and look upset. Ah, and now everyone's guffawing. I wonder what's so funny. I have no idea. But if I don't do the same as everyone else, they'll think I'm strange and cast me out.

Laugh. Laugh. Laugh. No, cry. Cry. No, laugh, you have to laugh.

I did my best to smile pleasantly at my parents, my teachers, my classmates; I acted the clown to make them laugh. Oh please, don't notice that I'm a monster who doesn't understand human emotion. I'll pretend to be a person so stupid they redefine idiocy, and while everyone is laughing at me and pitying me and forgiving me, please let me live on.

No one saw through my act, until I started middle school and met S.

Breathing raggedly, I ran up the stairs to the roof.

The third letter had been written not by Shuji Kataoka, but by Takeda.

How could I have been so stupid?

I'd only been able to see Chia Takeda within the bounds my common sense had dictated: as a silly, simpleminded girl.

Why had she been searching for S? Was she so obsessed with Shuji Kataoka's last moments?

I'd lacked the imagination necessary to understand.

Takeda's plump face, her wandering eyes, her childish mannerisms, her cheerful smile, her puppylike innocence, her singlemindedness, my desire to help her; I had seen only how they all appeared on the surface.

I'd never even considered that they could all be an act.

Why don't I tell you about S?

S was the person who understood me better than any in the world, was my nemesis, my best friend, my other half, my eternal opponent.

The terrifying wisdom S possessed penetrated everything.

My act, which hoodwinked everyone I ever met, failed to convince S.

I feared S accordingly.

The more fear I felt of S, the less I was able to escape.

In classes and after, I was with S.

I felt as though S's gaze was a judge employed by God to check me—a thought which caused my limbs to tremble and sweat to break out with fear and shame.

This world is hell.

I was a slave to S.

151

On my fourteenth birthday, S gave me a mug with a duck on it as a gift.

S told me that the duck's clumsy, stupid face looked exactly like me.

I giggled and agreed, and S glared at me, demanding to know if I really thought that was okay.

It scared me.

It pained S to think that I was a monster playing the part of a duck.

I rattled off a few jokes in an effort to reassure S somehow and appear lighthearted.

But S didn't laugh. S told me, "Quit it, Chee. I don't care if you're never anything more than a clumsy duck," and she stormed away.

I ran after S.

If S turned away from me, she might tell everyone that I was a monster.

I had to get S to laugh.

I had to stop her.

I would have preferred death to S leaving me.

As these thoughts ran through my mind, I let S see me fall in the middle of the road.

S turned back in surprise, then frowned in annoyed resignation and ran over to me.

Just as relief began to wash over me, a car sped toward us. S's slender body was thrown into the air, then fell to the earth and went still.

Shizuka Saito died to save a monster named Chia Takeda.

*   *   *

That day, when tender flesh was pulverized and red blood spread its tangy aroma across the black asphalt, I watched with an empty heart.
I had killed a person.
I doubt that God will ever forgive me.

I'm just an ordinary kid.

Even after I read No Longer Human, *I didn't understand.*

I'm just an ordinary, dumb kid, really, really ordinary, and so, so awful, so I couldn't understand why Osamu Dazai or Shuji would want to die, no matter how hard I tried. I read No Longer Human *five times. But I still couldn't sympathize with them at all. Finally, I just started to cry.*

What had been going through Takeda's mind, I wondered, as she told me that she couldn't understand *No Longer Human*?

I just started to cry.

What had she been thinking when she said that?

That's weird. It's deluded. There was no reason for him to ever suffer like that.
What had she been thinking as she spoke these words that cut into her?

I told the boy that I would go out with him.
He smiled, as naively as a puppy.

153

He had placed an innocent trust in me.

An uncorrupted, pure-hearted, gentle, happy white sheep beloved by God.

I envied him, was repelled by him, but at the same time I couldn't help but adore his simple effervescence.

But, perhaps, just such a boy might be able to change me.

They say that love changes people.

If so, that boy might be my salvation.

I might become a normal human being, rather than a monster possessing neither love nor kindness.

Oh, how I wish that I could.

I wished it so ardently that my heart seemed on fire.

Let me come to care for that boy.

Even if at first it's only an act, I know that eventually it would have to become true.

I replayed all the things Takeda had told me in my mind. They had mutated into new words with completely different meanings.

I had seen her look sad, like the day she had clung to me outside the school in the rain, or when I had told her that Shuji didn't exist as a way of hurting her.

But I had completely misinterpreted the source of that sadness.

I coddled the boy, smiling cheerfully at him and telling him over and over again how much I liked him.

It seems to have made him like me even more, but with each day that goes by I feel sadder.

Even when I continue my performance and seem the same as always on the surface, my spirit is like a terminally ill patient, growing ever more feeble and exhausted, and at times I experience suffering that torments my entire body.

One day when it was raining, the boy awkwardly touched his lips to mine behind the school building, and something burst inside me. It was not happiness; all the hair on my body stood up in antipathy.

I laughed for him shyly and told him I hadn't expected him to do that, then I ran away.

My mind was racing, and I felt a warm lump rising in my throat, pulling my nausea with it. I wiped my mouth off again and again and just kept running through the rain.

I hate it,

hate it, hate it.

I hate it so much. I hate everything, all of it, completely.

Why did my life continue after I killed S?

Shouldn't it have been the other way around?

Shouldn't I have been killed by S?

Hadn't I enslaved myself to S and heaped flattery on her because I wished for exactly that?

I hated S and also feared her. But deep in my heart, I wished she would destroy me.

Only S could have killed me; she should have!

But S is no more.

Unable to face the disappointment, the reproach, the rejection of others, too petty and fragile, I have no choice but to spend the rest of my life as a mime in order to fool the rest of the world.

That is a hell far more cruel and even further beyond salvation than the time I spent with S.

"I don't think there's anything wrong with being ordinary."

"I suppose…"

Why had I said something so thoughtless?

I didn't know. I hadn't known anything.

How much Takeda must have despaired, how it must have hurt her to hear me say, "There's nothing wrong with being ordinary."

I read a letter by someone very much like me.

It was like seeing myself. My heart was filled with it, and tears streamed from my eyes.

Finally, I'd met someone with the same spirit as me.

I was sure he would have understood my suffering and misery.

He inspired me to begin this letter.

I feel that as I write this letter, I grow closer to him.

It was not because Shuji Kataoka had something that Takeda lacked in her life, that she had been drawn to him so powerfully that she needed to discover the truth about his death.

It was not because he was her opposite.

It was because once she discovered that he had been created with the exact same soul that she possessed, Takeda had needed to find some proof of his existence.

I wonder who his S is.

How can I use S's weakness?

How can I move S's heart and drag out all of its secrets?

Only S knows about his last moments.

How did he die? Did he choose death for himself? Did S kill him? What did he whisper in his last moments? With what expression did he meet his end?

What answers had he found, this boy with the same soul as mine?

He will be my guide, whether I should live or die.
I have to know. Whatever it takes, I *need* to know.

I turned the problem over incessantly, but I stumbled upon the key to destroying S when I wasn't even looking.

As pain seared vividly through my chest like an iron brand, I finally understood.

Takeda and Shuji Kataoka were the same.

They both wished to be destroyed by a person named S, who was both their confidante and their enemy, and they had both lost people close to them through their own blunders.

They berated themselves unflaggingly for that, and it finally broke them.

Ever since losing her best friend, Shizuka Saito, Takeda had suffered only from her need for atonement. To her, Shuji's letter seemed like a map to escape her pain.

That was why Takeda acted as she had.

She brought me before the archery team alums and then sent letters to Soeda, whom she'd pegged as S.

Like poison falling—*drip, drip*—I watched with naked awareness on my face as—little by little—S went insane.

I can tell that S's usual ease has disappeared.

And that S's eyes are roving skittishly, and that S's voice is quavering.

Now and then, S has begun to sigh when no one is around and to tear at his hair, and to spin around to look over his shoulder in surprise.

What had been in Shuji Kataoka's mind just before he died, this boy who was her double?

How had he died?

Was it murder, or suicide?

Was he killed by another, or had he brought about his own death?

Takeda had needed to know that.

Whatever it took to do so.

Very soon.
My preparations are complete.
All that remains is to turn the key and open the door.

In order to decide her own future, Takeda *needed* to know, at any cost.

I have written a letter to S.

I'm waiting on the roof.
Let's discuss the truth.

On the last page of Takeda's notebook was written:

Shuji has given me my answer.
It's time to go to the roof.

Second floor—

Third floor—

Fourth floor—

The stairs seemed to continue up and up forever, and I was worried, terrified, that I would never be able to reach Takeda.

It seemed as though the farther up I went, the longer the stairs

became, and waiting at their end might only be an irreversible tragedy.

Wouldn't I just wind up standing there, watching without an inkling as to a course of action, as Takeda threw herself off the roof, like I had with Miu?

My heart was about to burst, and I felt light-headed, tempted to stop and rest.

It was no use.

I wouldn't make it there in time, just like before.

It was better not to go to the roof at all. I would only witness something I didn't want to see again. I would feel awful.

Don't go.

My lips and fingertips were tingling, my breathing animalistic, and white dots were swimming over my vision.

I hadn't had symptoms like these since starting high school. But when Soeda dragged me up to the roof, I'd been unable to breathe.

Just like last time, I was assaulted by a vicious hunger and unease; my entire body went cold; painful, whistling breaths escaped my throat; my body listed to one side, and I bent over the stair's handrail.

It hurt.

I was going to die.

I wasn't going to make it. There wasn't any time left. I shouldn't be going up there anyway. Everything about this was wrong. This situation was just going to make everyone unhappy. There was nothing to be done about it now. I was too late.

No, that's not true.

Just as I was being sucked into a morass of despair, an invisible hand took hold of my own and lifted me out of it.

Maybe it was Tohko's hand.

Tohko was the one who'd brought me this far, tugging on my apathetic hand and never giving up on me.

Tohko would never abandon me.

When I sobbed that I hated everything, that I didn't understand anything, she told me that I needed to find the answers to my questions on my own.

That even if it hurt or made me sad or tested me, I needed to get there on my own two feet.

Like Melos trusting in Selinuntius, I picked myself back up and sped recklessly up the stairs.

If it hurt or stung or my heart came close to rupturing or I couldn't catch my breath or my eyes clouded over, I couldn't feel any of it. I could only run toward my goal, my mind busy elsewhere.

At the end of the staircase I'd imagined might spiral on forever was a heavy door, and I practically threw myself against it to open it.

The May sky was as lovely and clear as ever.

Takeda was standing on the other side of the railing.

Her wispy frame seemed horrifyingly unstable.

"Takeda! Don't do it!" I shouted, running over, and she whirled around in surprise. When I saw the duck mug she cradled in both hands, my heart constricted with the certainty that she intended to die.

"Don't do it, Takeda. You can't kill yourself. It can't end that way! You're not Shuji! You're Chia Takeda, a totally different person! Just because Shuji killed himself doesn't mean you have to die, too!"

Takeda looked like she was about to cry.

I grabbed hold of Takeda's arm through the railing.

My shoulders heaving with each ragged breath, I snapped, "You have to find a different path than Shuji did!"

161

When she saw her rolled-up notebook in my hand, Takeda smiled ruefully.

"You read my notebook...didn't you, Konoha? I didn't want anyone to find it for ten years. It's a message to myself ten years from now. Just like the letter Shuji left for himself—for me—ten years later..."

"Don't be stupid. There's no reason you have to follow the same path he did. Get back here!"

Translucent beads welled up in Takeda's eyes. Her tears seemed to spring from the pain that her feelings would never be understood.

"But, Konoha, it would be too bitter and shameful for me to keep living. There's no other way."

Her restrained voice hid within it a scream of anguish, and it ripped into my heart, tossing aside anything I might have said.

Konoha, I don't think you would ever understand.

So I'm just repeating what happened with Miu, then.

"You know, Konoha, Shuji didn't die because he felt guilty about Sakiko's death. When that car killed her, he was disgusted with himself for not feeling even a hint of grief.

"I'm the same.

"I killed Shee.

"If I hadn't deliberately fallen down, she never would have come back and gotten hit by that car. So it's the same as if I'd killed her.

"But when Shee bled to death in front of me, it didn't awaken a single sad thought inside me.

"And I didn't cry at her funeral.

"It was more like I was in a daze.

"My family and friends and Shee's parents all thought it was natural since I'd watched my friend die right in front of me, and they said that I must have been in shock and sad, that I'd shut

down, that they felt sorry for me, that they needed to take care of me.

"But they were wrong!

"I wasn't sad!

"No matter how I searched my heart, no matter how hard I tried to cry by thinking about her, I couldn't find even a shred of sadness. Shee was dead, but I didn't care.

"That's...that's not natural! A person died! She was my best friend! It's not normal to feel nothing when that happens!"

Takeda's voice was growing erratic, and even more despair crept into her glistening eyes.

I couldn't deny that what she said was true.

In my mind, there was no question that it was abnormal, so I couldn't tell her otherwise.

I understood the fear of being different. But in the end, I was a spoiled child whose parents had always protected him. I had never experienced enough despair to understand Takeda's suffering.

"I'm not going to die because I feel guilty about Shee's death. Being unable to feel grief when she died made me ashamed, miserable, and afraid. That's why I'm going to die.

"It's just like Dazai said—even if I live, I will only compound my crimes with lesser sins, and my pain will only deepen and intensify! 'I want to die; if I don't, my life will be a seed for evil!' I can't go on living when I feel this way! Really, Konoha, do I have to keep on living like this? Are you going to tell me to live? That dying would be a mistake? Is it wrong for me to be at peace?"

My grip loosened on Takeda's arm.

In order to save Shuji from his suffering, Rihoko had granted him his wish.

But...

I...

I tightened my hand around her arm.

Takeda's eyes widened.

"I don't understand—I don't. Maybe I'm wrong. Maybe I'm saying awful things to you. But you really can't die. I can't explain why very well right now, but I'll help you find a reason to live! So please, just hold off on dying for a little bit! Try to live again! I'll help you think of something. We'll puzzle it out together! I can at least do that much!"

A tear slid from Takeda's eye. "Even that...it's not..."

"Please, Takeda. Come back here."

"No—I'm..."

Takeda shook off my grip. She lost her balance and wheeled forward, her feet slipping over the roof's edge.

"Takeda!"

Her duck notebook fell to the rooftop behind me and the wind swept through its pages.

I lay down on my stomach and grabbed one of Takeda's hands.

Both her legs and the hand holding the duck cup swayed like a kite caught in power lines.

"Let go...just let me die," Takeda begged, her voice rough.

"I won't!"

It felt like my arm was being torn off. I should have built up some muscles instead of spending all my time inside.

"Please, Konoha!"

"I won't!"

I wasn't going to let go—how could I? When Miu had dropped away right in front of me, I had just stood there, unable to do a thing.

I might not have been able to understand how she felt, or thought of the right thing to say, but I still could have run over and hugged her in my arms.

I could have reached out a hand and caught her.

So there was no way I was letting go this time!

"You can't die. There are lots of things that make people feel ashamed to be alive! Like two years ago, I was a girl and people said I was a mysterious young beauty and I was totally mortified. I stopped going to school and never left my house and I thought the future looked gloomy, but I'm still alive!"

Takeda's eyes widened, seemingly shocked at my sudden outburst. "You were... a girl?"

Just then, Takeda's hand slipped in my sweaty palm.

"Eek!"

Her hand was sliding out of my grip.

Two hands stretched out beside me and grabbed hold of hers.

"He's right. Everyone has something they're ashamed of that they try to keep hidden from people. Like how I was in the library reading *The Great Gatsby* just now and I accidentally started nibbling on it."

Tohko's flat chest was pressed against the concrete roof, her face scrunched in pain. Both of her arms stretched out to Takeda through the fence, holding her arm tightly.

I quickly steadied my grip on Takeda's hand with both of my own.

"Tohko? What are you doing here?"

"You want to know? When I went to the library, one of the girls there told me you'd bolted out in a big hurry... so I was looking for you."

Holding on to Takeda must have been pretty tough on Tohko, since she was even more indoorsy than me.

Bewildered, Takeda murmured, "You... nibbled on Gatsby? What does that... mean?"

Sweat pouring off her pale white forehead, Tohko replied, "Urf... it means there are a lot of things in this world you don't understand. Discovering those things is one of life's joys."

Suddenly there was a commotion below us.

Apparently someone had noticed us and was starting to panic.

Startled, Takeda looked down. Apparently realizing that she would lose her chance to die if she delayed much longer, Takeda started to shake her hand free. Tohko saw what she was doing and shouted, "Have you ever read anything by Osamu Dazai besides *No Longer Human*?"

"Huh?"

Tohko had caught Takeda off guard, and she stopped moving.

Pulling on Takeda's hand, Tohko began to talk with incredible urgency.

"There are people who only read *No Longer Human* and believe that Dazai's work is all dark, twisted, and depressing, but they don't really know what they're talking about. You can't judge all of Dazai's work based on *No Longer Human*. Did you ever read *Run, Melos!*? Melos goes to the market to buy something for his little sister's wedding, but he hears rumors about a corrupt king, and is overcome by his sense of justice. He goes straight through the castle's front door to kill the king and they capture him easily. Didn't you ever smile at hotheaded Melos? Didn't his powerful friendship with Selinuntius make your heart flutter? I mean, Melos runs back for him without any clothes on!"

Oh, what is Tohko talking about?

I wanted to hold my head in my hands.

But Tohko kept on talking, her face intent despite the sweat covering it.

"Just imagine it! No matter how the times change, it's always going to be embarrassing to tear through the middle of town buck naked. But Melos ran through town naked and reached his friend. And they redeemed the cruel, heartless, cold-blooded king Dionys!

"In the last scene, Selinuntius says, 'Why, Melos, you're

167

completely naked!' If I remember correctly, that line wasn't in my elementary school textbook, so you have to read the original! It's worth reading, if only for that line!

"And Melos isn't the only one. Dazai wrote lots of other wonderful stories full of love and trust in humanity! *Green-Bud and the Magic Flute* is a must! Your heart will ache with compassion for the girl who cares for her little sister when you find out she has an incurable disease. The last scene has a touch of gentleness to it in addition to the sorrow. There's light and hope. There's also the little sister in *Story of a Snowy Night* who wants to show her older brother's wife the beautiful snow-covered scenery, or the wife who feels a girlish devotion to her husband in *Heart and Skin*. They're all kind and innocent and lovable. The five brothers and sisters in *Roman Candle* make a collaborative novel together. Their family is as close as people on TV. And the girl in *High School Girl* is so adorable you want to hug her to bits.

"He wrote *Shame* based on letters that a female reader sent him, and *Goodbye*, which became his suicide note, but also *The Well-Dressed Prince* about a man who's obsessed with good clothing; that story has twisted images of people that are so rich with humor you can't help but laugh at them. You can see Dazai's rank humanity as he picks a fight with another author in the essay 'This Is How I Heard It.' If you prefer to be moved, you should read *The Pet Dog's Tale* or *Paper Money*! Those two are packed with Dazai's kindness and trust in humanity! They're both masterpieces that will break your heart. It would be a total waste if you died without reading any of those!"

What kind of persuasion was that?

Would an argument like that convince anyone not to commit suicide?

But Tohko was serious.

She was completely serious, desperate, giving it all she was worth, staking her life on it.

Though she gaped up at Tohko in shock, tears gradually filled Takeda's eyes until finally they spilled down her cheeks.

It had been so strange and ridiculous and overwhelming that she must not have known how to react.

Her face crumpled into an expression somewhere between laughing and sobbing.

Covered in sweat, her eyes bloodshot, Tohko continued talking desperately.

"Written under strict postwar censorship, his humorous collection of fairy tales is also a must-read. I was amazed at how he rewrote even the simplest stories.

"So, see? Dazai did more than just *No Longer Human*!

"Sure, maybe he died after writing it, and he wrote a couple other hopelessly depressing stories, and maybe he thought *No Longer Human* was the answer.

"But that's not everything that Dazai was.

"There are lots of kind, bashful people in Dazai's works. There are also lots of weak, ordinary people who become strong.

"*Setting Sun*, which he wrote about a bankrupted family based on the diaries of his lover Shizuko Oda, was the most celebrated book of its time. Even when the heroine's family dies and she loses her love, she gives birth to her child alone and tries to go on living with bravery. The last scene is nothing like a 'setting sun': it actually gives you the image of the sun climbing into the sky, shining proudly in the midst of a quiet morning setting! Even the sun that sinks below the horizon will rise again in a new day!

"You absolutely *cannot* die without reading the beautiful scenes he creates in *Golden Landscape*; the story is just as beautiful. You have to live at least long enough to read Dazai's complete works

cover to cover a hundred times and write a thousand-page report on them!"

The tears pooling in Takeda's eyes fell onto the hand that clutched her duck mug.

Slowly, she unclasped her fingers.

The cup plummeted to the ground and smashed apart.

With her newly freed hand, Takeda took hold of Tohko's—and my—hands.

Epilogue – A New Story

He told me I couldn't die.
That he wanted me to hold off on dying, because he would help me find a reason to live and suffer with me.

She told me I couldn't die.
That it would be a waste if all I'd read was *No Longer Human*.
That Dazai had written many other wonderful stories, and I had to live long enough to read them all.

They both appealed to me, holding on to my hand and arm.
I cried.
But I smiled while the tears fell.
Not understanding what I found so sad, so funny, so pitiful, so joyous, my tears simply streamed down my face. I couldn't stop them. My face must have been as slimy as a newborn baby's, or a monkey at the zoo.
My wet hand loosened and the mug Shee had given me slipped from my fingers and fell away.

I'd kept it where I would always see it so that I wouldn't forget the wrong I'd done to Shee.

But when I felt it leave my fingers and shatter on the ground, I was relieved.

My heart grew lighter, and I felt like I'd been freed.

Maybe that's because I'm heartless.

I am a monster incapable of understanding human emotions, after all, and maybe I shouldn't have lived.

Maybe I was supposed to end my life that day on the roof.

But I reached my hand out and took hold of theirs.

Their faces bright red, the two of them pulled me up in a chorus of grunting.

Partway up, teachers and firemen burst onto the roof and they helped put me back on the right side of the railing.

Later on the teachers and my parents all wanted to know why I'd done something like that. What in the world had happened? Was someone bullying me?

No, I climbed over the railing as a joke and my foot slipped.

It was *really* scary. I thought I was going to die.

I told them things like that while weeping piteously, and they scolded me for causing so much trouble.

Rumors flashed through the school, and I became famous.

There were people who gossiped about me behind my back, people who berated me to my face, and people who gave me sympathetic looks.

There were also some people who were kind to me.

And people who treated me exactly as they always had.

And concerned people who asked me, "Are you sure it wasn't a suicide attempt? Is anything bothering you?"

Each person responded differently.

There were kind people and mean people. And people who didn't care.

That's what school and society are like.

And I pretended to be a silly, innocent girl, laughing, "Heh-heh, I couldn't even do that right. How embarrassing."

Apparently it's not so easy for people to change.

I'll probably go on wearing my clown mask, deceiving the world.

But now I won't be ashamed of it like before.

I broke up with Hiro.

I told him that he must hate the way everyone looked at him when he was with me, and though he said he didn't, he looked away when he said it.

I think we need some space.

I sounded more cunning than usual when I said that, and he looked surprised, as if he were seeing me for the first time. He gave a quiet answer. "All right."

I know that Hanamura, the basketball team manager, has had her eye on Hiro.

Before, Hanamura would say mean things to me. So I'm sure she'll make him feel better.

And so the work of writing down everything that's happened isn't painful like it used to be.

Before, I was shining a light on the ugly, despicable truth about myself, and I turned my eyes away from the paper several times.

The stark black letters seemed like an evil curse, and they frightened me badly.

But now as I write, the filthy pus that had built up in my heart is being purged, and I feel purified. Writing calms me, and I feel as if I can glimpse a far distant future for myself.

I know that I will regret not dying that day.

But I will also be grateful to the two upperclassmen from the book club that I didn't die.

Of that I am sure.

Also, if I come across anyone who sees through my act, I intend to stand tall, laugh, and tell them, "You're absolutely right. What tipped you off?"

If I ever meet someone like Shee, I don't think I'll lie to them.

A week had passed since we'd pulled Takeda back up onto the roof. A steady June rain soaked into the trees.

Takeda had brought her finished report to us after school.

"Here you go. I'm sorry you had to wait so long."

Tohko had gone to the library, so I accepted the report in her stead.

"Whoa, this is really thick! You're a powerhouse."

"Heh-heh-heh. I ended up writing a lot. Hey, Konoha…you know how before, in the storage room, you said that writing doesn't change anything?" Takeda looked up at me, her eyes clear and bright. "I used to think so, too. But after I wrote this report, I realized that people actually could be saved by writing. I know it can happen."

"Yeah, you're right."

The stories Miu wrote always warmed me and made me feel purified. Miu had seemed happy, too, as she told her stories and wrote them down on loose sheets of paper that she kept in a binder.

I didn't believe that all of it could have been a lie.

So maybe it was possible to be healed or redeemed by writing, like Takeda said.

"That reminds me. Did you used to be a girl, Konoha?"

"What?! I-I never—"

"Up on the roof you shouted down to me that people used to call you a mysterious young beauty. Did you have some gender identity disorder, or were you a hermaphrodite or something? Or is it that you're gay?"

"Whoa, whoa, whoa! I mean, I—that is, well—"

"And Tohko said she ate a library book. What was that about, I wonder?"

"Uhhhhh, th-th-that was…I mean, we were grasping at straws! Just forget about it!"

Seeing me so flustered that my face glowed red, a knowing look came over Takeda's face and she smiled.

Maybe she was showing me her true self.

"All right. Everyone has things they'd rather keep hidden. I'll just lock that away in my heart."

"Thanks."

I was relieved. I didn't mind so much about my secret, but it would be a circus if anyone found out about Tohko. TV cameras and paranormal researchers would flock to her.

"Konoha, do you mind if I keep the love letters you wrote?"

"Huh? You still have them?"

Takeda gave me her old beaming smile. "Yeah. I put them in a pretty cookie box, where they'll be safe."

Whoa, that's a little embarrassing. But I owed her (I guess?) for promising to keep our secrets, so it wasn't such a big deal.

"As long as you promise not to show them to anybody."

"Heh-heh. They'll be my treasures."

Takeda asked me to say hello to Tohko for her, and said that she would come visit us again, then she left.

175

I sat down on a folding chair and started reading Takeda's report.

The sound of rustling paper mingled with the subdued patter of the rain falling.

It sounded to me like the gentle, pleasant rhythm of listening to a lullaby in my mother's lap.

Eventually the rain lifted, and the setting sun filled the room with golden light.

I wondered how much time had passed.

I'd been so absorbed in Takeda's report that when I felt something like a cat's tail tickling the back of my neck, I grabbed at it instinctively.

Huh?

It wasn't a cat. It was one of Tohko's braids.

I turned my head and saw that Tohko must have returned from the library at some point, because she had pulled a folding chair up and sat down directly behind me. She was leaning forward, reading the report over my shoulder.

Oh my God!

Tohko was staring intently at the report, playing with her lip with one of her fingers, looking utterly focused. She hadn't even noticed that I'd grabbed hold of one of her braids.

On the contrary, she leaned even farther forward, to the point that her cheek was practically brushing against mine. Her drooping eyelashes and the downy hair on her face glowed golden. Just a little bit closer and I could have turned my head and kissed her—that's how dangerously close she was.

"T-T-T-*Toh*ko!"

"Can you turn to the next page, Konoha?"

Amazing.

Tohko simply whispered into my ear, not the least bit flustered and never taking her eyes off the report.

"Uh, but..."

"Hurry..."

She was totally absorbed in it. Once she got like this, nothing could break her out of it.

A book girl's ears were closed to the world.

"O-okay."

I gave up and flipped to the next page of the report.

I could feel Tohko's breath, which smelled of violets, and the warmth of her body, and the soft hair of her braid tickling my throat as we read Takeda's report in the tiny room dappled by the deepening evening.

We finished reading about the time the soft golden light in the room had deepened to the red of evening.

Tohko let out a small sigh.

Then finally she noticed my bright-red face and the prickly tension in my nerves, and she jerked away.

"Uh—ack! I'm sorry!"

Since she'd thrown herself back so suddenly, her chair lurched and tipped over backward with a huge *THUD*.

"Oh man—"

"Owwwuh. I...I landed on my butt," Tohko whined tearfully. She'd hit the ground flat on her backside, revealing most of her thighs.

"Are you okay?"

"My butt hurts."

Tohko sat back up, straightening the hem of her skirt.

When our eyes met, she flushed with embarrassment, then quickly smiled at me with kind eyes.

"But I'm glad that little Chia seems to be happier."

A smile spread over my lips as well. "Yeah, me, too."

I grabbed Tohko's hand and pulled her to her feet.

I offered Takeda's report to her deferentially. "Your meal, mademoiselle."

Lit by the last rays of sunlight, Tohko sat with her knees together and legs tilted slightly to one side, her manners much better than usual as she accepted the report. "Thank you."

She grinned and paged through the report, starting over again from the beginning.

Each time she finished a page, she tore it out and began nibbling demurely at its corner.

"Bleh," she murmured, a somewhat forlorn expression coloring her face. But she chewed methodically, taking her time before swallowing. "It's really bitter…"

The report probably had very little of the sweetness or tenderness that Tohko had been expecting.

She continued to eat away at the bitter, bitter report philosophically, though I was sure there couldn't be much of it that was palatable.

Tohko's pale skin, her school uniform, and her long braids were all caught in the bewitching, yet somehow forlorn colors of the setting sun.

On the roof, Tohko had told Takeda that the sun that sinks below the horizon would re-emerge in a new day.

No matter how awful or painful something may be, a new and different day would surely come.

And perhaps in repeating this process, people changed as they moved toward a new day.

The pain you never thought could heal might eventually fade.

I hoped that somewhere Miu was smiling, though she had leaped to her death that day.

Even if I could never see her again, she was somewhere under this mellow evening sky.

All things pass away.

I opened my packet of paper and wrote.

Over the faint crinkling of paper as she ate the report, Tohko asked, "What are you writing?"

"I'm not telling."

"Konoha...you should write a novel sometime. You'll let me read it if you write one, won't you?"

Tohko said it so suddenly that my heart jumped.

When I looked up at her, she was smiling placidly.

There was no reason to suspect Tohko knew the reason behind my blush.

So it was probably just another of her ramblings.

Tohko went back to her meal. I continued scratching words onto the paper.

I didn't know if the day would ever come that I could write another novel, or if the day would come that I wanted to.

But today I would write something sweet for Tohko, to be her dessert after she finished Takeda's bitter report.

Afterword

Hello, Mizuki Nomura here. This new series is the story of Tohko the book girl and Konoha, the once-brilliant young author and the mystery girl.

I wanted to try something that went in a different direction from other series I've done in the past, and after much discussion with my editor I put pen to paper. We talked about making a serious story, and in the earliest premise Tohko was a much more distant and bloodthirsty character. But once I started writing, she ended up being the exact opposite and turned into a happy-go-lucky girl, so we branded it as a "bittersweet comedy" in the promotional material.

Wait...comedy? Well, look...you can't say that there aren't *any* comedic elements, and...um...it is serious. Just so you know!

Warmly despondent—that's the kind of story I hope it will be.

Now, like Konoha, I had only read textbook excerpts of Osamu Dazai, the author that Tohko discusses at great length in the story. A friend of mine in high school whispered that "Reading this book makes you want to kill yourself." That left a big impression on me and I thought, "Wow, this book must be cursed!" and I stayed far away from it. But during the writing of this book, I

read a handful of Dazai's works and my image of him changed completely. I'm a convert. I can recommend any of his short story collections, so those of you who haven't read him should pick one up.

Illustrations for this series were provided by Ms. Miho Takeoka. Her dreamy use of color, so transparent and ethereal, truly took my breath away. Tohko is exactly as I had pictured her and I got emotional when I saw the sketches. Thank you so much for your amazing drawings, Ms. Takeoka!

Each time I begin a new series I worry whether I'll make it to the end of the story. I'm going to do my very best, so I hope you'll come along with me! Bye for now!

—Mizuki Nomura
April 4, 2006

Hello, I'm Miho Takeoka.
Ms. Nomura entrusted
me with Tohko and
Konoha, and I've finally
managed to get them
into their uniforms
and find their books,
papers, and
school bags.

Did you forget
anything, kids?

I would like to
extend my thanks
first of all to my
editor, but also
to the designers
and printers.
We couldn't
have done it
without you.

SKETCH FOR
AN ALTERNATE
COVER IMAGE.

SPICE
&
WOLF